Scunthorpe Revisited, Added Articles and Instant Relatives

Scunthorpe Revisited, Added Articles and Instant Relatives

SPIKE MILLIGAN

Edited by Jack Hobbs

MICHAEL JOSEPH
London

MICHAEL JOSEPH LTD
Published by the Penguin Group
27 Wrights Lane, London W8 5TZ, England
Viking Penguin Inc., 40 West 23rd Street, New York, New York 10010, USA
Penguin Books Australia Ltd, Ringwood, Victoria, Australia
Penguin Books Canada Ltd, 2801 John Street, Markham, Ontario, Canada L3R 1B4
Penguin Books (NZ) Ltd, 182–190 Wairau Road, Auckland 10, New Zealand

Penguin Books Ltd, Registered Offices: Harmondsworth, Middlesex, England

First published in 1989

Made and printed in Great Britain by Butler & Tanner Ltd
Filmset in 11$\frac{1}{2}$/13$\frac{1}{2}$pt Times by Butler & Tanner Ltd
Frome and London

A CIP catalogue record for this
book is available from the
British Library

ISBN 07181.3356.0

Dedication

This book is dedicated to the people of Scunthorpe, some of whose relatives from all over the world can be seen scattered through these pages. Among the missing Scunthorpe relatives not depicted here, are – Clark Gable, Dick Plunger, Gengis Khan, the Aga Khan, the Aga Cooker, Terry Wogan, Pheasant Plucker, Desmond Morris, two Rottweilers and a Partridge in a Pear Tree.

Contents

Foreword

'Oh dear, oh dear, oh dear.'

Those were the very words of the proofreader on reading this book. He said to Jack Hobbs and myself: 'What are you writing this stuff for?' We said: 'To make people say – oh dear, oh dear, oh dear.'

He shook his head; we could hear the bits rattling inside. 'I'm sorry but this book baffles me,' he said.

'Oh dear, oh dear, oh dear,' we said.

He looked at us and said, 'For God's sake, what's the book about?'

'I don't know,' I said. 'We wrote it but we haven't read it.'

'Oh dear, oh dear, etc,' he said. He told us that no one at Michael Joseph understood it. I nudged Jack Hobbs. 'Oh dear, oh dear, etc,' he said. The proofreader opened the proofs and flicked through the pages and groaned.

'Look,' said Jack Hobbs, so the proofreader looked and Jack Hobbs played our master card. 'This book is Ayatollah-proof. If the English people won't understand it, it will baffle him. Don't you see, this book was written to save everybody at Michael Joseph from being assassinated. Salmon Rushdie would love to have written this.'

The proofreader seemed unimpressed. Jack Hobbs held his head still and smiled. 'Those people are instant relatives.'

The proofreader wearily took his glasses off. 'Where are you?' he said.

'Here,' we said.

'I can't see you,' he said.

'I think the prescription on your glasses has run out,' smiled Hobbs.

ix

'That's better,' said the proofreader putting them back on. 'Now what are instant relatives?'

Jack Hobbs told him that instant relatives arrived much quicker than other types. 'Some relatives are non-instant and very slow,' he pointed out. We all looked out but there was nobody there.

'So what's in this book for the reader?' said the proofreader.

We said, 'It's a chance to say "Oh dear, oh dear, oh dear," and then read on. With regard to the articles, the book is so bound that any article the reader doesn't like can be clipped out. This will help the book to become lighter. The best method for disposing of the discarded pages is to refer to the Society of Goatkeepers, contact one of their people, take the discarded pages to them, and they will get a goat to eat them for you. On the other hand you may be an environmentalist, in which case you can post your discarded pages to Friends of the Earth who will pulp them and have them made into trees. Now about the photographs. If you don't like them all you need do is paste some black paper over them. All this done the book should now be acceptable and you can stop saying "Oh dear, oh dear, etc".'

Antiques

That's nice, I thought, the Editor of *Antique* phones my Manager and says, 'Can Spike Milligan write an article for *Antique*?' She said, 'Is that autobiographical? I mean he's seventy.' 'No no,' says Editor, 'not necessarily. He can write anything he likes provided it's on antiques.' 'How many words?' said my Manager. 'Could he manage 800?' 'Oh no,' said my Manager. 'He only knows 356. If you want 800 he'll have to use some of the same words twice.'

So here I am. I do/have collected antiques but at a time when they were cheap. The bug first bit me in 1940 when my regiment were billeted in Worthingholme in Bexhill-on-Sea. It had been a girls' school but the school had been evacuated in a hurry, leaving behind a whole library of books piled up in the attic. Among them I found two volumes of *Gells Pompeiana* 1835, bound in leather and indented with gold lettering and beautiful copper-plate engraved illustrations. It was this which suddenly opened up the door for me to find an interest in classic antiquity.

This was compounded during active service in the Italian Campaign when I actually visited the excavations at Pompeii during the eruption of Vesuvius. I even went digging along the perimeter and found a delightful Samian dish which now, at pre-dinner drinks contains peanuts. And that's what I got it for – peanuts (eh???). As my regiment advanced up through Italy I had access to cities like Rome, Florence, Venice and Ravenna, so I was exposed to wondrous antiques.

We move to the post-war years and my hunt for antique bargains. One of the strangest occurred during a visit to Dinely Studios in Marylebone, the onetime London home of Charles Dickens where he wrote several of his books including *David Copperfield*. With traditional indifference the Borough Council were letting it be

1

Terence Throttle playing pocket billiards
accompanied by his dog and his wife.

demolished. I was looking for souvenirs and I managed to get some porcelain doorknobs. Now, everytime I enter my withdrawing-room my hand touches the same knob as Charles Dickens'. But this wasn't the end. At the rear of Dickens' demolished home was a large block of Victorian flats, now being razed by a giant iron ball crashing into its walls, and there, exposed on the fifth floor, was a full size grand piano. Quickly I bribed the site foreman with five pounds if he could get it down. The money did the trick and the piano was lowered to the floor in a net. Another ten pounds to have it transported to my home and *voilà* I had a grand piano. It was a straight-ended Broadwood with casework of saw-cut rosewood on mahogany ground work. I phoned Broadwoods with the serial number, 21813. Yes, they had a record of it, made and sold in 1883 for £140. For a complete overhaul and restoration I took it to Robert Morley's of Lewisham. It cost £400, but when I asked them the piano's current value they said £3,000, so who's a clever boy?

There is a haunting quality to antiques especially if passed down through the family. In this respect I had two unexpected 'finds'. I knew my grandfather had a sister, Annie Milligan. One day I received a letter from a lady who said she had in her possession a sewing box with the inscribed name of Annie Milligan. It was indeed my great aunt's, who *was* a seamstress. It fills me with a sense of wonder that this box had survived nearly a hundred years. That it is in my possession now is a small miracle.

My next find was equally fortuitous. At a BBC Christmas party I met a Mr Sutton who kept a warehouse of antiques which were used by the BBC for dressing sets. In course of conversation it came out that my grandfather had the unusual name of Kettleband.

'That's strange,' said Mr Sutton. 'I've got a mirror in my Woolwich warehouse which has a label on it with that name.'

I visited the warehouse and there on an overmantle mirror was a worn buff label with the faded inkwriting 'A. H. Kettleband', Alfred Henry Kettleband, my grandfather!! Sutton told me the mirror had been deposited back in his father's day, about 1900. That would have been about the time Alfred Henry Kettleband, who lived in Jackson Road, Woolwich, was called up for the Boer War. Mr Sutton sold the mirror to me for £50.

'I won't charge you for the storage,' he laughed.

The mirror has a haunting quality. How many times did Alfred Henry Kettleband pause to straighten his tie, comb his hair ... Ah, yesterdays, for God's sake someone tell me why I get such a thrill from this. I suppose collecting is like saving something from drowning in the past.

My next find; it was Christmas and I was appearing at the Mermaid Theatre in *Treasure Island*. Every night my homebound journey took me past the boarded-up Bedford Theatre at Camden Town. One night, along with a torch and a book of Walter Sickert's paintings, I ascended the dank stairs and, finally, lining up the paintings with the stage I found what must have been the exact seat he had sat in to paint them. That's all. It was a straightforward journey into nostalgia. Finally, I toured the dressing rooms; they had all been vandalised

Fireman Ocker resting during a conflagration.

4

and the mirrors smashed. I opened the door to dressing room number one on stage level and flashed my torch. It was a miracle: there was the mirror intact with its original frame, the faces who'd looked into it, from Marie Lloyd to Laurence Olivier. I salvaged it and gave it to the Mermaid Theatre for installing in *their* number one dressing room. It is now in the possession of Bernard Miles.

Another theatre story. We were filming at the old Wilton Music Hall in Grace Alley. During the lunch break I was poking around in the rubble under the stage when I came across a strange object: a piece of galvanised tin, about ten inches long by seven inches wide, round at the top and curved, with two metal prongs at the bottom (see illustration). Suddenly, it hit me that these were the footlight shades. I found another ten and I am glad to say that they are now on display in the London Museum.

Another strange find was a street in Queen's Park where a terrace of Victorian houses was being demolished. I noticed that above the door of one house a large iron fireback was affixed to the wall. Borrowing a site ladder, I removed it and took it home. Embossed

Wilton Music Hall footlight shade.

on it was a cockerel clutching a sea serpent together with the date 1652. The mystery was solved by Sir John Lambert who informed me that it was, in fact, to commemorate the war of the Fronde in France. How it ever got to where I found it will remain a mystery. Most certainly it is a rarity.

Eight hundred words!!! I really must stop. Editor, the money please.

Christmas by Christmas by Christmas

Ho ho ho ho! Those sons of fun, flesh and finance, the Directors of *Penthouse,* have in a moment of disorientation, commissioned me, Spine Millington, your friendly district visiting rapist and plumber, to write 2,000 words on the season of Christmas. So far that's forty-eight!

Christmas, as the consumer society knows, is inflicted on the world of shopping, starting anytime after July, with warning signs in windows – Only one hundred and fifty shopping days to Xmas! Christmas is not in the Jewish calendar so it's in places like Golders Green that signs of the first plastic holly appear. Like that appalling house cladding it starts to spread up through filthy Finchley, wacky Whetstone reaching my area of barmy Barnet by August. Signs like 'Join Our Christmas Club Now' appear in morticians' windows. Come September and coloured brochures from every charity from Battersea Dogs Home to Send a Boot for Christmas for Single-Legged Parents are all selling Christmas cards. October and November, and sure enough, like the ghosts of Belsen, the early turkeys start appearing in the poultry shops, line after line of plucked ghastly white bodies with a sprig of plastic holly around their necks, supposed to promise seasonal good cheer to those who can eat the corpses. TV adverts show great bulging oven-ready turkeys, too big even to fit in a wardrobe let alone the average oven, and the man telling you 'Booti-ful, real bootiful.' I tell you, I've seen hundreds of dead turkeys, none looked 'bootiful'. Gad! Can anyone imagine anything less seasonal or Christmassy than having to plunge pounds of prunes, walnut and

6

sage gunge up the stricken animal's bum? There is something wrong with us all!!!! I am a vegetarian and enjoy my Christmas with a carrot and apple and a plate of yoghurt wearing a paper hat. Early December, and the nation slaves over hot Christmas cards. Again the threatening warnings: 'Last post to Australia December the some-think!'

Oh the pressure, we're all starting to enjoy ourselves!!! Everywhere skint households are raiding children's money boxes, electricity money, the gas meter, forcing Granny at gunpoint to hand over her pension. The buying of seasonal alcohol is immediately penalised by the news that 'ten thousand extra police are being drafted in to breathalise suspected motorists'. At sorting offices extra staff are taken on to burn the thousands of children's letters hopefully addressed to Father Christmas.

Travel agents are imploring British citizens 'Fly to Hong Kong for Christmas for as little as three thousand pounds.' Great! Flee! Run away from your own people, avoid giving presents, avoid bloody relatives, yes happy Hong Kong. You arrive on Christmas Eve after crippling confinement for twenty-four hours, zonked out and smashed on cheap alcohol and totally jet lagged. By the time you've slept it off, lucky you, Christmas . . . has gone!! Melly Christmas . . .

What of the unemployed who are looking forward to their dole money with a sprig of misletoe attached? At the Job Centre life is stirring. Strolling actors of no fixed income, no visible means of support (no braces) are searching the Job Vac boards for signs asking for hohohoing Father Christmases for shopping precincts, from Tescos with false beard, to Harrods asking for retired gentlemen with real beards. All this, but a part of the Christmas scene. Jesus has a lot to answer for.

Christmas in India 1923

My own particular memory of Christmas was more fragrant: it had curry smells. My first recollection was when I was four and living in the Cantonment of Poona, a well-known wog beating area. In the

Nan King, a chambermaid, feeling a couch with the permission of her mistress – Lady Eleanor Clench.

baking heat of 120 degrees in the shade I observed my parents sticking little blobs of white cotton wool on the windows. Never having seen any, I never knew it was meant to be snow. On reflection, how much more appropriate to have dotted the windows with curry paste and slicked banana portions.

My little questioning mind asked my parents how Father Christmas came and was told 'Down the chimney'. When I pointed out we hadn't any they changed tack. Ah yes, no, this Father Christmas would come via the back door. That's why they left the back door open, and that, dear reader, is why we were burgled. Alas, the thief, being a Hindu, had no idea that in the early hours my parents would be actively placing the presents at the bed end. They both collided in the parlour, my father grabbed the thief, naked except for a loincloth, while my mother phoned the police. Hearing the noise, I and my brother arose from our beds to see turbanned policemen manacling and hitting the unfortunate Hindu with their fists until he apparently told them he was a Harijan (Untouchable). When they reverted to sticks, the Hindu fell to his knees clutching my father's legs.

My little brother said to me, 'Is that Father Kwismus?' I didn't know.

Seeing us, my mother shushed us back to our beds with the story that a naughty man had tried to steal all Father Christmas's toys, and on that we went to sleep again.

I tell this story because the following year, by which time the family were in Rangoon (The Rangoon Show), come Christmas my little brother said, 'Are the hitting men coming tonight?'

My mother, who had forgotten the incident, said, 'What hitting men, dear?'

'You know, Mummy, the hitting men and the man with no clothes on who cried!'

Should she take him to a child psychiatrist? No, no hitting men came that year. Instead, at five minutes to midnight on Christmas Eve, the earthquake came. My parents leapt from their beds and rushed us into the garden as the crows, disturbed from the trees, sent up a great cawing. Yes, that was another Merry Christmas.

Lulu as a child with her novelty foxtrot
'I've just kicked the bucket'.

Christmas 1944

I was a Lance Bombardier at an observation post on the forward slopes of Monte Sperro in Italy. With me was Lieutenant 'Johnny Walker' and his assistant Bombardier Eddie Edwards. It was Christmas Eve, the rain fell in sheets, it was icy cold and we sat in our slit trench sitting on wooden boxes with water slopping around our boots. We took it in turns to try and empty out the water in a small tin. As darkness fell a man from the battery scrambled down the slope; it was mail from home!

'Bombardier Milligan?'

'Yes,' I said.

'Nothing for you,' he said with a cheery laugh (the bastard). One letter for Walker (lucky bastard).

By a covered torch he read it aloud: 'Oh my God,' he said, 'I've been burgled.' We couldn't help it, we laughed.

To add to the festive cheer a German 155mm gun started to lay down harassing fire; we tried to doze. As it drew near to midnight an infantryman from a nearby slit trench must have watched the clock reach midnight and started to sing: Silenttttt nighttt (CRASH BOOM A SHELL) Holyyyyy nighttt all is peace (WEEEEE BOOM!) Round yon manger (WEEEEEE BOOM).

The last one landed just above the trench and threw up a column of mud that descended on us. By the light of the torch we saw that Lieutenant Walker had got it right in the face and, looking like Paul Robeson, said, 'Hello dere! A Werry Merry Christmas.'

Ah! They don't have Christmases like that anymore.

Peter Sellers' Rolls-Royce Christmas

Christmas Eve 1959, the children were asleep, the wife and I had filled the stockings and likewise lay asleep. The cat was asleep, the canary was asleep, best of all my bank manager was asleep. At two in the morning the phone rang: it was my lunatic friend Peter Sellers.

'Spike,' he said, 'Please come round right away!' and hung up.

11

Noting the urgency in his voice I pulled on an overcoat and in pyjamas drove to his house, 'St Freds' in Oakley Avenue, Whetstone. When I arrived he was sitting in his new Rolls Royce Camargue with the engine running. At first I thought he was fleeing one of his numerous wives, but no.

'What's the trouble? It's three o'clock in the bloody morning.'

'Three Little Girls from School are we'
sung as a solo Chinaman.

He waved me aside. 'Spike,' he said, 'You are a true friend.'

So far, I thought.

'You see, this is a brand new Rolls Royce, and there's a squeak in the boot.'

'Thanks for telling me,' I said and prepared to leave, but no.

'Wait,' said my looney friend. 'By day the squeak is barely discernible but now at night when it's quiet it should be easier to locate.'

What *was* he getting at?

He continued. 'Take these,' he said, handing me a piece of white chalk and a torch. 'I want you to get in the boot then I will drive along the streets. I'll bump the rear wheels up onto the pavement to agitate the springs and increase the noise of the squeak.'

I'll cut the story short. I thought, I've come so far so I may as well go the whole hog. I climbed into the boot and he locked me in. We proceeded to drive the district, I, on my knees in the boot, making little white crosses where I heard the squeak. Suddenly the car stopped. I heard crunching footsteps (it had been snowing), there was mumbled conversation. A police patrol car had seen this Rolls bumping up and down on the kerb and pulled it over. They had listened to Sellers' (also in his pyjamas) explanation. To verify it they now opened the boot to find an unshaven tousle-haired man in the boot in his pyjamas on his knees drawing little white crosses on the floor.

The policeman shone his torch full in my face. 'Oh,' he said. 'It's *you*.' Merry Christmas.

Christmas 1959

On Christmas Eve 1959 I placed a recording machine in my children's bedroom after I turned the lights out. Alas, at one stage the machine broke down but this is a verbatim record of my three children's conversation, Laura aged seven, Sean aged five and Silé aged three and a half.

Laura: We must hurry up and go to sleep.
SILENCE

Silé: Did you heered dat, dat was me being quiet for Farder Christmas.

Laura: Shhhhhhh, I can hear someone coming!

Sean: It's not me, I'm already here.

Laura: Shhhhhhhhhh, Sean!

Sean: I *am* shushinggg, listen . . .

SILENCE

Silé: Do bunny rabbits have Quickmass?

Laura: Oh hurry up and stop talking.

Sean: It wasunt me, I stopped talking ten hours ago.

Silé: Dat wasunt me talking, dat was Sean.

Laura: Father Chrismis won't come if we are not asleeped.

Silé: Doesn't he like awake children?

Laura: Yes, but only if they are asleeped.

Sean: I'm asleep now but I can still talk.

Laura: (CALLING) Dadddyyyy . . . Daddyyyyyyyyyy.

ENTER FATHER

Me: What is it?

Laura: They won't go asleep.

Me: Listen, children, if you don't go to sleep Father Christmas won't stop here.

Sean: Where will he stop?

Me: Oh, er somewhere else.

Sean: I wish we lived there.

Me: Now be good and go to sleep . . . Goodnight.

OMNES: Goodnight, Daddy.

SILENCE

Silé: Shhhhhhhhh – I think he's coming.

Sean: Tell him not yet I'm still awake.

Silé: So am I, you can hear me being awake.

Laura: (DESPERATE) Ohhhh, go to sleeppppppppp. Go to sleeppppppppppppp.

Silé: I'm *going* to sleep, listen.

SILENCE

Sean: I can't hear you.

Silé: I'm sleeping with no noise.

Laura: Sean! Silé! Go to sleep.

14

Silé: I can't go to sleep as quick as you, 'cause I'm smaller.

END OF TAPE

Merry Christmas, Folks!

Leonard Dicks, the mormon, after marriage.

My Country Right or Wrong

My country right or wrong – well, it took me some fifty years to find out which country I was right or wrong about. These days, a true ethnic heritage is hard to find: to what and whom do we owe allegiance? I mean in the multiracial world we now have, with the increase in, for instance, black sportsmen appearing in our football teams, it's not impossible that the entire England team could consist of black players. So these days we tread a fine line as to what race we belong to – as to what *country* we belong to.

I remember meeting a red-headed green-eyed man in a Sydney bar. He said his name was Patrick O'Brien. When he said he was Australian, I wanted to tell him (like in the USA) that Australia was the name of the company. He was an employee. Ethnically, he was Irish, and he being extant was due to his being carried in the loins of Irishmen since the coming (pardon the pun) of the Irish. Unless we recognise our ethnic origin, patriotism doesn't make sense.

The identity of one's country reached high levels of absurdity when Japan attacked Pearl Harbor (it was in all the papers). There were some 1,000,000 Japanese people in America, and from them a Japanese division was formed. Fortunately, they were spared the pain of fighting Japanese troops by being committed to Italy, but it has all the ingredients of farce. Witness one 'Australian', Dennis Wu of Chinese descent who fought the Japanese on the Kokoda trail and was, until taken out of the line, shot at by *both sides*.

All this I had to consider before deciding what country I owed my allegiance to. I was born of pure Irish stock on my father's side

*Norman Castle and his bicycle trapped
in a photographer's studio.*

(O'Maolagain, O'Higgins, Kennedy), on the distaff side Kettleband (English) Burnside (Scottish). Being born in India added a further dimension (more later), so with that Irish–English–Scottish mixture I could reasonably call myself British. All my family were Indian Army, back to the Mutiny, so my formative years were 'British'. Patriotism was shown by always standing for the national anthem and being a little white sahib one felt a little superior. Only one touch of Irish surfaced – a lot of fights in the playground and every 17 March, my mother would pin on a green ribbon token of St Patrick (and *he* was Welsh! Help!).

The first dim adumbrations of seeking grass roots was reading of the Easter Rebellion of 1916 in Dublin, and feeling uneasy about the execution of the leaders. Then I realised my Irish father behaved differently to other fathers who were plain and boring and English. No, my father told me incredible tales about himself, from how he and his brothers (six) fresh from Ireland in the 1900s were set upon by bully boys (a penny, a pin or a punch) to winning the Battery light heavy championship – to shooting tigers. I personally saw his prowess as a superb horseman, trick rider's dressage. Again, he was a wonderful tap dancer, singer, actor – from him flowed an endless stream of wonderful tales – fighting Arabs in Mesopotamia in World War One, to being a cowboy on the Bigh Ranch in Brownsville, Texas. This was pure Irish fantasy that springs from the minds which created Leprechauns and Banshees, so finally, I decided he *wasn't* British but Irish, while I still remained British, as I did until the war came and went. I was pleased that, like my father, Montgomery, Alexander and Conningham were Irish.

Then I started writing the 'Goon Show' and as it was so different from other British shows I wondered why – most certainly, my Irish father's fantasies had had their effect on me. I read *Finnigan's Wake*; I felt at home with the book. I read 'As I Was Walking Down Sackville Street' by Oliver St John Gogarty and I thought I felt a shift in emphasis from being British to Irish.

It wasn't until 1963 that I decided to test my Irishness by writing a novel about Ireland, bearing in mind I had never been there. I wrote *Puckoon* on the basis of my father's personality and stories – it became

Filthy Fluter's Ball.

a bestseller and I became more Irish. I flew to Dublin to launch the book there and there and then I realised that I *was* Irish – it meant new allegiances. I didn't cheer the English Rugby Team – no, now it was all Ireland. Eamonn Andrews lent me two giant volumes on the history of Ireland – wow – the potato famine, after that how could anyone cheer the English.

The final transition for me was an asinine law that relieved me of my British Passport. It was a bit of a trauma being British while you were still Irish, but 'You are now stateless' says a chinless wonder Passport Officer.

Enraged, I phoned the Irish Embassy. 'Could I become an Irish Citizen?'

'Jasus yes, come round right away we're short of people.'

I was what I always should have been. I had found my grass roots (like Alex Haley who went mad when he discovered he'd been adopted). I wanted to go to where those executed for the Easter Rebellion lay. One Autumn day, alone, with a high wind filled with leaves and a Celtic grey sky pregnant with rain, I made my way to Arbour Hill where lay the Irishmen who had given *part* of their country's freedom, and I surprised myself by weeping. All those false years were shed in a lachrymose moment. I was 55, I was Irish, this was my country right or wrong.

I cannot but end with a postscript from the Home Office, September 1988: 'Thus in the normal course of events, someone in your position would expect to have become a citizen of India.'

So next, Spike Milligan the Hindu?

Collecting for Collectors of Collections

Alan Coren, the born-again editor writes me: 'We have a collection special coming up, I thought you'd be just the bloke (BLOKE???) to write a thousand words etc. etc.' (so far, Alan, 30) so would I? I phoned my Manager and told her to say yes. As I was phoning from the Finchley Labour Exchange I thought this was a good answer. I recalled the last time *Punch* asked me to write for them, I was alive.

Collecting. To start you don't need much money; first decide what you want to collect, a knowledge of antiques, their re-sale value, where to find them, and how to break in.

Portobello Road is a collectors' paradise. My brother bought his valuable collection of Georgian silver cutlery there. At first the vendor asked the absurd price of three hundred pounds. An astute bargainer, my brother bartered with him. Finally he knocked him down. Before he could get up, the silver and my brother were gone.

One of the most common collectors' favourites is coins. Coin collecting can be fun and financially rewarding, anything from one pence up to one pound coins, the higher the denomination the more valuable the coin. I've been collecting them for some time now. Some supermarkets are willing to accept them instead of the standard credit card. People have shown a great interest in my collection – my bank manager, my baker, my butcher, my grocer, the list is endless. Among the most avid coin collectors are James Goldsmith and Robert Maxwell.

Edible jig-saw puzzles are a good collectors' item but hard to find. Rarer still are Taiwanese Turin Shroud tea towels, likewise clockwork

'Three Little Girls from School are we'
as a trio.

Hong Kong Virgin Marys that whistle Ave Maria every hour on the hour. Space is a problem with collectors. This is solved by collecting miniatures as they don't take up much room and can be drunk at leisure.

Among the most obsessive of collectors are the Egyptologists and those authorised tomb robbers – the archaeologists. The greatest collection of Pharaonic gold ever discovered was that of Tutankhamun, found after a lifetime's search by Howard Carter. Even then he was frustrated. When he prised open the entrance to the tomb, it was too late: the young Pharaoh was dead. The most outlandish of all collectors must be the late lamented murderer John Christie of 10 Rillington Place.

His collection now rests in Scotland Yard's Black (coloured?) Museum, where, neatly laid out on cardboard sheets are snippets of pubic hair from all the women he slept with, all neatly labelled, e.g. 'Doris – 3 March, 1951'. Like all collections their value will appreciate with time and no doubt one day appear at Christies (coincidence?) as a job lot under ephemera. On the subject of pubic hairs, edible jigsaws are a good collectors' item but hard to find.

The unluckiest collector was the late Robert Groynes, who after the war foresaw the dramatic rise in the price of antique collections. With this in mind he disguised himself as a vicar and drove around rural Dorset collecting 'any old furniture for the poor of the parish'. In a blinding stroke of luck, a farmer showed him a priceless Louis XV commode being used as a roost in a chicken pen.

'Yew can 'ave 'ee,' he told the delighted Groynes who dashed off for his van, during which time, the farmer had to saw the legs off to 'get 'ee out of pen'. The eggs Groynes found in the drawer were no compensation. The Judge's verdict: 'Suicide while the balance of his mind was disturbed.'

My father collected guns. My father was Irish, and when applying for a licence, the police asked what kind of guns. He said, 'Ones that go bang.'

Running parallel with Christie was the grisly Victorian practice of collecting shrunken heads. One such was Captain Lewis Tuffington who purchased several from Dyak Indians in Borneo, only to discover

A terrible day in Scunthorpe.

to his horror that one was that of a missionary. Dutifully he forwarded the head in a jar of preserving fluid to the grieving widow with a sympathy card imploring her to 'accept it in the spirit in which it was sent'.

Unique among collectors was Frenchman Louis Thing. Blind from birth he collected braille pictures of naked women.

One of the most profitable forms of collecting is wine. My own personal hobby is collecting wine, and my other hobby is opening it and drinking it immediately.

Naturally, I go to auctions. At the last one I bought a veneered walnut wardrobe. You have to have something to keep your clothes in and as luck would have it this something turned out to be a veneered walnut cupboard. Wine, vintage wine, is a sound investment, though I personally have never heard it making a sound. However, some wines are best drunk when young and with this in mind I started at the age of fourteen. A good collectors' wine is Chateau d'Yquem. 1947 was a great year. I should know; that was the year I slept with the bird with big tits from Brockley. I think the rest of her came from Brockley as well, but I digress. No, vintage wine should be laid down and drunk immediately. It's a known fact the collectors improve with drinking. You see, today a bottle of La Tache would cost you £25.00 whereas in twenty years time it would be worth £60.00! – an increase of £35.00! So it's best to drink it while it's cheap. If, as in my case, your wife finds you face down drunk on the floor of the cellar and says, 'My God! What did you get drunk for?', you can say, 'Twenty-five pounds, a saving of £35.00 and you didn't have to wait twenty years.'

On the subject of wine, jig-saw puzzles etc. etc. (1,000). In cash please Alan . . .

Tom Mange, a Scunthorpe ventriloquist, rehearsing.

Wildlife

To the World Leaders (pardon me laughing), two major problems occupy their horizon: (a) The Western World, The Arms Race, and fear of death by Nuclear Incineration, and (b) The Third World (what happened to the second) in fear of death by starvation. The former is still a prospect, the latter a reality, but it's the H-Bomb that gets the headlines.

Philosophically the H-Bomb is only as terrible as you and the media make it. In terms of the individual, no matter how big the H-Bomb, it can only kill you once. Therefore, it has only the destructive power of a blow from a stone-age axe, or being run over by a London bus, so stay cool. Yes, it can destroy whole cities. Again, we destroyed whole cities by 'conventional' means in World War II – Hamburg and Dresden – why, then, the horror? It's mainly the prospect of the unknown. An Atomic War would release the capacity to destroy *ALL* major cities in a nation. OK, but it's the aftermath, not the death rate, but the total breakdown of the infrastructure of our lives, *sans* government, *sans* law, and the outbreak of survival by barbarism and savagery – in other words, like World War I. No one dreamed of what was to follow in the slaughter fields of the Somme, but the memory of that occasion must be the ghost that haunts us in that *NO ONE* knows what a post-Atomic War holds for us. Even as I write, I wonder will I be shooting my neighbour to stop him getting at any food I will have remaining.

Question: why have we invented and go on 'improving' this almost fictional weapon? Milligan's Law: the size of weapons increases in

27

relationship to the size of the population. I mean, who is going to drop an H-Bomb on a village of 200? No, there's got to be enough people to kill, otherwise its *not economical* you see.

What's this all got to do with wildlife you say? (For that is what I've been commissioned to write about.) Well, in England we have no wildlife of any substance: the Deer, the Badger, the Fox, and that's the list of our 'Big Three', all three persecuted, despite various 'protective laws'. Illegal Badger digging, and Badger baiting goes on apace, the result of laws with no teeth. As for the Fox, killing him is a 'jolly day out' on the Sabbath.

I'm going to point out now that areas of the world where the real wildlife exists are (at the moment) fortunately not in the Atomic firing line, i.e. South America, Africa, Burma, New Guinea, the Arctic and Antarctic. They are 'safe' from immediate Atomic impact. However, they are still in a gradual state of decline, and every year species become extinct. Since 1900 (and slightly before), some men (among them Teddy Roosevelt) with the ability to see and think ahead (themselves a dying breed), realised that flora and fauna on this planet were being exterminated. The reason was man, not man as such, *but too many men as such*. That is the root and continuing cause of the destruction.

Attempts to conserve the dwindling world of nature were set up by well-intentioned men around the world, and there are groups of people desperately trying to save Wildlife. The method in the main is to shut off areas, and pronounce them Conservation Areas. Will they succeed? For the time being, yes. In the long term, Wildlife, except on a very minor scale, is doomed; the reason is unchecked population growth.

A small example. In Rwanda there dwelt a herd of elephants in what at one time had been a vast area which afforded them room to forage. In the last few years unchecked population grew around them until they were literally surrounded, and were forced to maraud local farms. The Government decision? Shoot them! Fortunately, some Conservation Groups came to the rescue, but only of some. They air-lifted out a few of the young bulls and cows in helicopters. The rest were shot! The rescued elephants were flown to a comparatively safe area, but the statistics of the venture are this: by the time the young bulls and cows have reached maturity the Rwanda population around will have closed in on them and the 'shoot them' situation will be repeated. This time there will be no young bulls or cows to lift to safety. This is just a microcosm of what is happening *everywhere* in the world.

Homo Sapiens all believe, and act, as follows: 'We are the most important creatures on this planet, anything that stands in the way of our survival must perish.' This is the thinking not only of the man in the street, but Governments, *and,* I would venture, most conservationists. With unchecked population, and this kind of thinking, even an idiot must come to the conclusion that at some time in the future the Wildlife holding areas will be swamped if not legally, then by force, or sheer weight of numbers. Needless to say, if I thought that man was in such small numbers that his existence on this planet was threatened, I would be concerned. As it is, there is absolutely no shortage of people (the opposite, too many), so my feelings are now solely for the cause of animals. I am saying to the Conservation bodies, your efforts are, in the long run, wasted unless at one and the same time, you run a parallel programme of population stabilisation, and then reduce it to a level where man and nature can live side by side enjoying each other's mutual benefits. The thinking should become part of Government Policy. At the moment, most World Leaders are environmental ignorami.

A shining example of a leader who was an environmental idiot was Chairman Mao. 'Have lots of children,' he told his people. An environmental disaster has followed. The current Chinese Government have suddenly woken up to the size of their population, and the threat to the future. One thousand two hundred million when they took the Census in 1983, and even as they added it all up, the figures were *out of date* as *three million* were born while they were counting. They now know that, unchecked, by the year two thousand they will start to starve. The Draconian action they have taken need never have happened had they listened to Malthus. They now have the situation where people are forbidden to have more than one child; it is a social *crime,* and mothers are forced, or coerced, into aborting a second child.

You would think that the World Leaders would look at this result

Leonard Clench hiding it.

and say 'Hey, we can avoid this', but are they? There are looneys who tell you that Britain's birthrate is (a) stabilised or (b) falling. Utter Balls. Population Concern will tell you we will increase by a minimum of one million by 2000 AD, and unless you are daft you must realise that one day we will have a population of a hundred million. Even as I speak, the DOE are trying to turn Green Belt into building land. You can't blame them, because there's a need for more houses.

I was one of the blind ones, never gave a thought to having four children, when I was complaining about the traffic jams getting worse. It didn't occur to me that four of the cars in front of me were *my* children (how to make your own traffic jam folks!). In this country we are 56 million; in 1800 we were only 11 million. The difference is that at one time you could walk down a London Street in a straight line. Have you tried Oxford Street in shopping hours? Aye, there's the rub, the change is so pernicious, a child born today expects to be crushed in the tube trains, stuck in traffic jams, never able to swim the length of a local swimming pool without crashing into people every three feet. Up to a year's wait to get into a hospital for an operation (unless it's life and death).* I know doctors who work four days and nights in hospitals non stop and as for 'we must build more houses', how many bloody years have the Governments and Councils been saying that? Marxists who rail against capitalist exploitation never mention the fact that capitalists can only exploit the working class if there is such an abundance of labour that they can pick and choose. Reduce the numbers of the working class to a size where *they* can pick and choose their employer. (Just a thought.)

No, I see no long term hope for the world of Flora and Fauna. I myself realise that to be a true conservationist you should (a) be a non-smoker (b) only have two children (c) be a vegetarian, and (d) do not own those two creatures that are anathema to wildlife: the cat and the dog, and of course that just about excludes 90% of Western man. Still there's always Disneyland (Helppppppp ...) Me? I'm off to queue for a ski-lift holiday in Austria.

---

* Just today a friend told me his father has been waiting 18 months for an operation for a new hip joint.

31

'Three Little Girls from School are we'
as a quartet.

Australians at Play - Beach Life

London. England. The phone rang. It's my Manager.

'Australia are on the phone,' she says.

'Thank God,' I reply. 'At last they can communicate with the World.'

'No, no, no – no jokes,' says she. 'Kevin Weldon & Associates want you to write an article on Australians at Play.'

I tell her the last time I saw Australians at play they were all out for 109. No, no, no – Australia at Play – Beach Life. Beach Life? OK.

Well, I said, there's crabs, thank God I've never had them, horse flies, seagulls and a few ice-cream papers. That'll be ten dollars, or six in cash.

No, they want 1,000 words – 1,000? there aren't that many! but here goes.

Beach life. I don't know anybody who has spent their life on a beach – however, there are beaches in Oz – my own experience was in that Jewel of the Pacific – wondrous wave-washed Woy Woy. In summer you can't see the sea for people; in winter you can't see the people for the sea. Ah, those beaches! Ocean and Pearl beach – its wonderful shallow waters make safe bathing for kids. I know, I tried to drown my little buggers, but it was too shallow.

If you can't afford the train fare to Woy Woy, there's Bondi. Bondi is a well-known resort – to me, a last resort. In the high season avoid Bondi like the plague. In fact, if plague broke out in Bondi it could only help.

Christmas Day 1979 there was no room in the water. It was full of

Kiwis over here living off Australian dole. Thank God they've got Shark nets – it's the only thing that stops the poor creatures being trampled to death. But – Ah! – there is a jewel of a beach ten minutes across the Rip Bridge at Woy Woy. It's at the back of the late Tass Drysdale's home – Maitland Bay. Now there's magic – not many people visit it – because it's a half-mile hike down a deep incline. Few people make it to the bottom; even fewer make it back again. I tell you, the bodies I passed on the way down.

This beautiful bay is where the now deceased Kurangi and Dharug tribe used to fish and collect crustaceans (you look it up, I had to) off the spit of rocks that runs out to sea at the north end. Here too are the rusting remains of the SS *Maitland,* after which the Bay is named. She was wrecked there one dark night in the late 1890s during a trip from Sydney to Newcastle (I think it was smuggling John Singleton's money out). The bell of the ship is now in a small stone memorial on the road above the Bay.

The Bay is a sweeping curve of sand hemmed in by the surrounding high bushland which hides it from human eye. Some days when the Pacific is like a mirror, snorkelling among the rocks is great for youngsters (attended by Dad, of course). You do get the occasional vandal. One of their tricks is to steal all the loo paper from the beach dunny – a crime that should be punishable by death. For voyeurs in search of topless beaches, well it is pretty like any beach. I've seen old ladies with binoculars peering out of windows at the topless men swimmers at Patonga.

Now there's another getaway beach – Patonga, once an Abo burial site. It is now, or rather was, a place for retired members of the *Sydney Morning Herald* and the Commonwealth Savings Bank. In the 1950s I remember the big event was the annual retired Bank Manager wheelchair race on the beach. By 1970 they had joined the departed Abos and homes were going as weekend retreats to trendy Sydney Solicitors who were introducing windsurfing. During the course of an hour I watched one bloke fall off thirty times and I couldn't see the point of it at all.

What I am saying is Australia at Play or Beach to me has always been the Central Coast. It's getting a lot more crowded since I first found it in 1956, but there is still time before Yapoonism reaches there. What's Yapoonism, you say? Well, in Australia there's another country called Queensland – The Queen is Beolk Petersen. In that land there are people who can count up to twenty (here go my Brisbane bookings). My friend Ray Barrat lives there because he says it makes him look intelligent. Now, in Queensland is a place called Yapoon – miles and miles of empty beaches – but along comes a rich son of Nippon who says to Queen Petersen, 'Ah so – we make amends for making you build Burma Railway – we buy all Yapoon – and make it into Billion Dollar Oh Boy – hello, sailor – Disco Casino – like Las Vegas – and Australian Tourists allowed into sea free.'

As my friend Ray Barrat said when he heard the news, 'I'll have a cup of tea, a Bex, and a lie down.' The locals didn't like this so there is now a 'Come-and-blow-up-bits-of-Jap-built-disco-package-holidays' campaign.

Oh yes, there's a lot of fun in Australia. But wait, by golly, I forgot – Islands – the ultimate getaway – well, I thought it was getaway. I had the offer – a freebee on Dunk Island – ah, paradise! – peace. We land on a dirt air strip – looking good. The airport is a grass hut – looking real good. But – what's that emanating from it? It is what you can get in any mainland supermarket – piped muzak – worse – I'm offered (in good faith) a champagne cocktail – help! Where's the peace – the coconut milk? We are shown a very splendid hut – amid trees – lovely, perhaps I was wrong. I spend the afternoon resting from a three-month One-Man tour. Dinner is in a nice large building – some 100 diners, all behaving, and I've a pianist – lovely very civilised, seafood good – my Ben Ean is chilled – then – HELP!

I'm set on by a sunburnt crone, with a downmarket Dame Edna voice. She plonks in my lap, shoots the soup all over the table.

'Owareya!' she yells. 'I'm from Woy Woy too, I know yer muther! Hey!' she calls across all the crones from her table. 'Lookooittz! Spine Millington – the one yer see on the television.'

No, not all islands are islands – Robinson Crusoe would have left this one.

But not to worry, there is Magnetic Island, beautiful and for history freaks. A short boat ride from Brisbane takes you to St Helena Island,

35

onetime Penal Colony with substantial ruins still there. Fossicking on the beach found me a Queen Victoria five shilling piece.

Look, I could go on writing about Australian beach life – look, it's simple, the beach runs all the way around it – get in yer car, pick yer spot – its bonza! It's so good I'm coming back this April, bail me Mother out of Woy Woy Jail. Woy Woy, that's the town – it's so small the local Hooker is a virgin. So hurry while stocks last.

'Three Little Girls from School are we'
done by dogs.

Racism

My name is being defiled, I tell you. Murdoch's Mucky Dailies have printed that I have been put on the Black List for appearing in South Africa. Fools! Most people in South Africa are black! What got me laughing was reading the American Showbiz Bulletin *Variety: Shirley Bassey* on Black List. No, but seriously, folks! Some of my best friends are Jews, but some of my very best friends are black Jews.

So what is the crime, me Lord?

That you, Spine Millington, did, with malice aforethought, etc etc journey to The Cape, and did willingly make *white* people laugh.

Laughing in white!

Nay, your Honour! Let the truth be told through the ancient pages of the this-week-we're-not-on-strike-*Times*!! This is how it goes.

In 1974 during the building boom (when you consider the noise of a cannon's boom, and worse the Sonic Boom, why is the building boom so silent?) all I heard was the wailing of the developers when the fringe banks collapsed. I actually have an oil painting by Monet (Monet is the root of all evil) of a fringe banker collapsing, a magnificent sight. No, but seriously etc, you see my meagre semi-detached was suddenly very important in that they were pulling the street down to build high-rise flats (the population in England is falling, ha ha ha), so a developer offers me hundreds of thousands of pounds or he will exchange my sem-det. 2 up. kit. bt., Grg. Gdn. for a Mansion in Hertfordshire. So we did a straight swop, but the mansion, once in rambling acres, (*See Dia A*) was now all subdivided (*See Dia B*).

It was now a piece of land *à la* postage stamp. Behind me was a

A miserable woman accompanied by a Lance Corporal.

A 'Jim'll Fix It' group photograph.

DIA. A

ME

Mansion

in

HERTFORDSHIRE

Before Developer's Subdivision

sign: building plot for sale. Dead centre was a beautiful Weeping Ash and on the border a superb Copper beech, Milligan thinks: those trees should have a Preservation Order on them, so I contact those balls of fire the Barnet Borough Council. And lo, they speak and say, Yes the Copper Beech *has* a Preservation Order, but, ha ha, *not* the tree in the *middle* of the plot (the Ash) ...

Second letter: 'Why is the Weeping Ash, which is rarer than the Beech unprotected?' They answer (wait for it), because of its *condition*. Gadzooks! is it pregnant? I call unto me those fellows, Men o' the Trees; who inspect the Ash with the sort of loving care a Dutch Jeweller would handle the Hope Diamond. They talk of the tree as 'her'. 'She's orlrite, fact is she's un beauty, nought wrong with her.' I pass their observations to the Barnet Borough Council, but they, like the sons of fun they are, insist *their* expert is *more* expert than the Men o' the Trees.

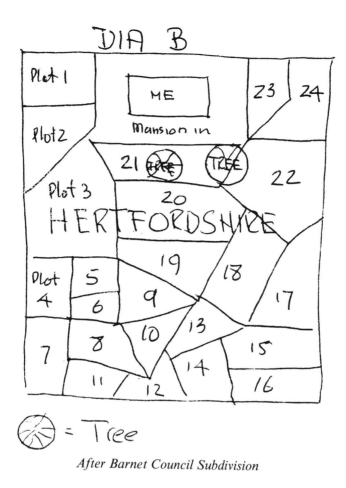

After Barnet Council Subdivision

Then it occurs to me that the Copper Beech itself might be in danger, and the Barnet Council agree that it is 'possible' the Beech Tree will have to be sacrificed but that would be compensated for by re-planting. I can't believe it! They defy the Trades Description Act. Preservation does not mean *chop down,* nor re-plant. So, I'm faced with the task of saving the trees. How much is the land? The Vendor, friend of mine says: 'Spike, it's £50,000 but in cash £15,000.' We settle for £12,000, but I haven't a penny, but ha ha, here come de judgement day.

A South African Entrepreneur has been making me offers to go to the Vile Fascist Country, so Fascist that it has a Jewish community nearly as big as England's (quick! pen and paper, write: 'Dear Sir, How dare Spike Milligan say, etc etc etc). The offer to appear is exactly £12,000, so, I went there, making sure that my contract stated that I appear for 'multi-racial audiences'.

I made sure that I always took the coloured stage staff to a restaurant after the show (as food tasters, of course). They were a bit amazed telling me it was 'whites only', but no one objected, only the blacks who said 'what are all dese whites doin' in heah?' No one seemed to care. I went and did a show for the Asian community, did a couple of gigs for coloured schools, went to Soweto on Sharpeville Remembrance Sunday (I had to get a permit). I was the only white person in the Church and the Vicar asked me, 'Are you from de Police?'

The crux of it all was that with the £12,000 I bought the building land: with Fascist money I saved two trees from destruction by English bureaucracy, so these jokers, who can't wait to put the finger 'Racist' on you, might at least investigate the circumstances.

No one from English or American Equity has ever written to me asking *why* South Africa. I could give them some very good reasons, like I can get work there, but not here, like I think I'm a good actor, a funny man, and a clown to boot, yet in my thirty-six years in show business, I've very rarely been offered any stage work. My first offer came at the age of forty from Bernard Miles to play Ben Gunn. The second and only play I was ever offered was by Michael White in Oblomov. But for the fact that I am an author, I would have starved to death; this is not a cry of pity, just a statement of fact.

For the *Guinness Book of Records,* I must be one of the rare people who've never been offered a Summer Season, or a Pantomime. Fortunately the BBC have always given me periodical TV series, and let me have my head (they also allowed me to keep my body, legs and teeth), so it's no good these jokers pointing the finger of racism at little old Spike Milligan. How about Nat West? They're appearing there every week and a lot of Equity Actors bank with them.

Howzat? Out?

My Home

It was 1951. I was young and green in my years and I sang in my chains like the sea. The flat my wife and I occupied suddenly started to shrink; this was caused by the unexpected appearance of two children, a dog and a stray cat – the last two I don't know about, the children were apparently mine.

'We must get a bigger place,' said wife.

'Infanticide is cheaper,' I said.

A house. We started what all Britons will know as the most agonising time of one's life. For the next year we scanned the columns for a home. We visited house agents – their names became more familiar than Hollywood stars, names like Benham & Reeves, Knight, Frank & Rutley, and Chestertons.

Those who answered the phones in these establishments became Gods – they all sounded like Battle of Britain Pilots in between scrambles. 'You'll go to what? – £3,900 (He made it sound like you were a Mega-Scrooge) and that is your final offer.'

'Yes.'

Then, in tones in which doctors tell of a terminal illness, he'd say 'Oh dear.' He would conclude with that old favourite: 'I must warn you' (like a boxer with a low blow) 'that there are several offers already in the pipeline.'

'Are they higher?' you drivel. No, he's not at liberty to say, breach of etiquette. You wait a day, two – three – four – five – after a week you can't stand it.

'Hello, remember me.'

One more cornetto, give eet to me.

'Who? Oh, you want Mr Gibbs-White. He's on holiday, can I help you?'

You go carefully through the whole sombre story.

'Ah, yes – 29 Clens Avenue – I'm afraid it's gone.'

'Gone!? You – he – never told us.'

There follows a standard apology. New Secretary – phone out of order – World War III pending. So passes six months. We are now well and truly on the books – circulars cascade through our letter box arriving on a Saturday morning. We race around North London to see 'Delightful Edwardian Home: 3 bed. 2 sit. Kit. Bt. Gr. Gdn. In need of decoration'.

The outside is peeling, and not just the paint – the bricks – the front garden was once, I suppose, a garden – weeds – vestiges of a pebble path – caravan – a jacked-up Ford Zephyr – and dog shit – several ageing 'For Sale' signs almost invisible with weathering (two of the Companies have gone into liquidation).

'It might be better inside,' says wife.

'I'll top that,' I said. 'It's *got* to be better inside.'

Monday 9.00 a.m. 'Hello, 127 Holden Road – could we make an appointment?'

The agent with all the enthusiasm of a Rabbi at Nuremberg Rally says: 'I think that can be arranged.' I want to say, would you feel better if I knelt down?

We saw the home. It was terrible – but it was better than this continued enslavement to house agents and – *ah!* SURVEYORS – 'It's not worth buying – it's got dry rot – damp rot – damp course gone – needs re-wiring – re-roofing.'

'You forgot leprosy,' I said.

The grovelling, cringing, paying and signing of documents went on for months. In mid-contract the owner died of a stroke – a stroke of luck for his wife. He left her £50,000. She now wanted the price of the house raised. I was now on tranquilisers, and would sign any-thing – money didn't matter – one had to escape from the enslavement of the system. I put the deposit down in 1951. I was in the house for twenty years, nineteen of those it was still the Building Society's. I

45

called the home 'The Millstone'. In February, 1971 I paid the last instalment – now, it was *mine*.

Despite the Surveyor's Report condemning the house – he didn't know (or find out) the house was built on a spring. One day the floor in the cellar burst and filled to four feet. The children loved it. To cap the spring would cost £2,000 – or as the builder said, 'We can contain it by digging a well, but you'll have to bail out with a bucket when it floods.' I re-christened the house The Titanic. I sued the Surveyor, but he was too clever for me – he died.

The roof. In 1957 there was an incredible gale. The whole roof tiling fell apart. The insurance policy, yes, there it was, full cover for storm damage. The assessor arrives. 'Ah yes, you need a new roof,' he said. 'Have you had a builder in?'

'Yes and rain.'

'Ah – £1,500 for re-roofing, I'll go over this at the office and let you know.'

A week past – two – three – rain poured in – we slept in a tent in the bedroom. I couldn't wait; I told the builder Ernie Stevens go ahead. He started by putting waterproof sheeting in the attic. The dripping stopped. It was quite something to hear an approaching scream from above – and for a workman to hurtle through the bedroom ceiling and crash to the floor by the bed. It was Ernie's mate Ted. He was unconscious. We had the ambulance. It rained that night especially through the new hole.

'I need a couple of hundred up front for more scaffolding.'

I never saw Ernie again. I got another builder, Mr Dick Soames, but his price would be £300 more. I phoned the Samaritans six times that week. Dick Soames mended the roof. He took six months, during which the Insurance Company joker said they would meet a *fifth* of the cost. A fifth? But it says storm damage. Ah yes, but that's only for buildings built after (in small print) after 1932, provided the roof gables were double latticed, dove-tailed, one made by a Chinaman during the Equinox of the moon only visible in The Easter Islands.

I'll sue! I brief my solicitor.

'Don't do it, Mr Millington, you'll lose the case, it would cost a lot in legal fees – like this advice, £35.00. Yours etc. Jim Solicitor.'

46

I was now forty. I *owned* my own home, on eight Tryptazol a day, three Secanol at night. As I write, my wife is bailing out the cellar. Tomorrow I'm registering the house as a ship.

Ann Cleethorpes, an overweight lady jockey with a terrified horse.

A cholera victim in full dress.

Another Christmas

Something must be rotten in the state of Denmark (*Hamlet*). Something must be written in the state of Yorkshire (Milligan). Yes, the Editor of the *Yorkshire Post,* with his mind obviously in a deranged state, phoned up my Agent, (who I thought had gone down on the *Titanic*), and said of me: (a) Is he alive, (b) if so, is he confined to a wheelchair, (c) can he still write?

My Agent's answer: (a) yes (b) yes (c) yes.

Then, can your man write 2,000 words on the subject of Christmas, in a merry season vein.

Oh yes, says my Agent (herself deranged and in a wheelchair). What, in God's name, is there funny about Christmas – the whole build up to the damned thing is sheer agony!

The *best* Christmas I had was 1940. England faced a rampaging Germany across the English Channel. Poised along the French Coast were highly trained Nazi troops with formidable Mark IV tanks, and even more formidable 88mm guns. Facing them in an OP on Galley Hill, Bexhill-on-Sea was Gunner Milligan with a Canadian Ross Rifle, plus five rounds of ammunition, that even now he was groping for on the floor. It was 24 December, a dark night as Gunner Milligan lit a Woodbine to add to the Seasonal Festivities.

Two thousand years past at this very hour, a young girl called Mary is giving a roasting to a middle-aged Jewish chippy. 'Why didn't you book a room when I first told you.'

'Darlin, I tried, but these bloody Romans are given preference over the Jews.'

'You needn't have said we were Jews, you could have said we were Irish.'

'Irish, with this nose, no, listen, I know what I'm doing. Who's going to report the birth of a baby in a hotel, eh? No, but ah! ah! baby born in a stable – that's news! – you just believe me, darlin.'

So, thought Gunner Milligan – as he sat staring into the inky blackness of the Channel – five hours to midnight. All around the Christian World, millions of seasonal victims were putting up green prickly leaves, with red poisonous berries. Other sex mad people were hanging up white berries to trap some poor innocent female victim and give them appalling halitosis kisses. Other poor creatures were on their knees, wrapping presents covered in sticky paper and knotted string, at the same time holding the door shut from screaming kids. Others, pouring with sweat, are stuffing turkeys, geese, chickens – and in poor families, sparrows, mice and worms. Some poor devils are trying to get large turkeys into small ovens by using grease and mallets. Other victims have already started to roast their bird – sleeping by their ovens, with a tube from the oven up their nose so they can smell burning. Some actually sleep in the oven alongside the dinner.

So, thought Gunner Milligan, four hours to go.

Meantime, 2,000 years ago Mary is going at Joseph. 'Listen I'm not having that baby with that Donkey and Cow in the room.'

'We got to keep them – in the lease they are down as "central heating".'

'Oh! Why me God? Why me?'

Gunner Milligan thinks, surely Hitler wouldn't invade on Christmas Eve? Just in case, Milligan looks up his German Dictionary, there it was – *Frohe Weihnachten*. So, his duty was simple. If a German arrived, you hailed a piece of mistletoe, and said *Frohe Weihnachten*, then shot him.

It was evil, but not as evil as my brother Desmond's 'Christmas Games for Perverted Children'. In a wartime utility England, he had invented a cheap game. For this game you needed a dear old Granny. First you hid Granny in the linen chest on the landing (but gag and bind her so she won't give the game away). Lock the lid. Then you say, 'Mummy, Daddy – Granny's hidden in the garden (we know it's a lie, but it makes the game last longer). After a month you say, 'Mummy, Daddy, do you give up?' and they will say 'Yes'. Then you show them where she is. And the game is over. Next, the Police will come. You will say, 'Merry Christmas Officer,' and they will take you away, and you'll never have to work any more.

So, thought Gunner Milligan: 2000 hours – four hours to go. Milligan raises the D5 phone and buzzes the Command Post, and a drunken voice answers.

Voice: Command Post, answer.
Milligan: Who's that?
Voice: I only wish I knew – ha ha ha ha.

Joking apart, Gunner Milligan is serious. He has to report every hour, on the hour – all quiet – or report anything suspicious.

Milligan: Listen, can I speak to the Duty Bombardier?

The answer is an hysterical drunken laugh, followed by what sounds like violent retching.

Christmas Eve, three hours to go. I sat in the little Observation Post, made tolerable by a one-bar fire we had run from a local Fisherman's cottage behind us, the Billet for the other OP.

I recall the first Christmas I could remember: India, 5 Climo Road, Poona, it was 1923 – I was five. I had awakened and 'caught' my mother and grandmother placing a pillow-case full of toys at the foot of my bed.

'Where's Father Christmas?' I said.

Unprepared, Mother said, 'He's just gone back up the chimney.'

Even aged five, I thought she must be mad. We didn't have a chimney. I said so.

'Mummy's joking,' said a stammering Scottish Grandmother. 'She means the window.'

This excuse was even weaker – the window was covered in chicken wire.

'Did he get through one of the holes,' I said.

'Yes,' said the Scottish Grandmother with a sigh. 'Now go to sleep.'

51

A BUPA victim.

God, is there any greater joy than a child seeing his toys on Christmas morn? I can still see that box of British lead soldiers – eight Grenadier Guardsmen with Captain, the shiny scarlet tunics, seven with rifles, one with a sword. I ate my breakfast with them on the table. They stood around my plate at Christmas lunch, and again at tea. By oil lamp I packed them into their box and they slept by my bed. Those soldiers! They have marched through my head ever since.

So, thought Gunner Milligan, now here was I a *real* soldier. No red tunic, but an outsize Khaki Battledress, still reeking of anti-gas impregnation. No – oh, no – who would want to gas a Battledress on Christmas Eve?

What did we do on Christmas 1939? I was twenty-one – by day, a bouncing semi-skilled fitter in Woolwich Arsenal, by night a scintillating Trumpet Player in Tommy Bretell's Ritz Revels. A band of spotty lads, held together with Brylcream and pimples. We lived at 51 Rosenthal Road, Brockley Rise, SE4. Staying with us was my Uncle Hughie Kettleband, a bandsman on leave from the Royal West Kent Regiment. He was love sick for a girl called Ruby and was about to bring disaster to the Season.

I was in the bathroom shaving my pimples, my brother Desmond was 'playing cowboys' with Uncle Hughie. They are using my Father's *real* Army pistols, and unbeknown to us, Uncle Hughie has put a real bullet in his gun. The plan is to shoot himself in the foot by 'accident' and – guess what – Get out of the Army. To remedy the situation, covered in shaving soap, dressed in a vest, with braces dangling, on a freezing winter day, I ran all the way to Dr Costley's. The nurse stared at me.

'It's an emergency,' I gabbled.

'Is it you?' she said, backing away.

'No, my Uncle has shot himself in the foot. We think he's bleeding to death.'

We return in the Doctor's car, an ambulance arrives, the neighbours congregate as Uncle Hughie is carried out. I don't know why but as he went we said 'Merry Christmas.'

We spent Christmas morning at Lewisham Hospital. Owing to the pain, Uncle Hughie had been given Morphia. Having ruined our

53

Christmas, he lay there, grinning and singing (God knows why) 'When the blue of the night meets the gold of the day'. We stuck it for an hour, then my father said 'Let's bugger off.'

'What a good idea,' said Mother.

We got back in anticipation of resuming the festivities, but were greeted at the door by a Police Sergeant.

'Sorry to disturb you, sir, but we've been informed by the Lewisham Hospital of a gunshot wound.'

'Merry Christmas,' we said as we filled in Police Forms.

But in 1940, there's someone out there approaching in a car. Germans – surely not – they were supposed to come by sea? Two figures debouch. I take a grip on my rifle. 'Halt who goes there – friend or foe,' I shout.

'Friend,' is the reply.

'Name the password,' I call.

'Checkerboard.'

'Advance and be recognised.' I still didn't recognise him. 'One at a time,' I add. A figure approaches. My God! It was a General wearing a camel-hair overcoat. 'Can I see your identity sir?'

Without speaking, he handed me his Officer's Book, I checked the identity photo – a hook-nosed man with a Ronald Coleman moustache. The name General Alan Brooke meant nothing to me. I returned it.

He spoke. 'What do you do?'

'I do my best, sir.'

'The way things are, it might not be good enough.'

He questioned me as to my duties. I explained it was basically to report any German arrivals on the coast. I didn't know I was speaking to the man who did as much – if not more – to win the war as Churchill but then again, he did not know *I* was Spike Milligan.

'I know it must be pretty galling to be doing this on Christmas Eve,' he said, 'but you should get satisfaction knowing you are doing a very important job of work.' He seemed genuinely concerned. He asked about my family. 'Do you smoke?' he said.

'Yes, sir, when I can afford them.'

He called to his driver. The driver approached, carrying a card-

A child molester and his family.

board box. The General dipped in and produced a packet of cigarettes. 'Merry Christmas,' he said and departed.

Jesus got incense and myrrh – Gunner Milligan got twenty Players.

One hour to midnight. Joseph to Mary: Look, darlin, can you keep the groaning down? The neighbours are complaining.

I smoked one of the Players. It was very quiet. Most Players' cigarettes are quiet. I should hate cigarettes that emitted noises – who wants a cigarette that barks – of course, if they sold fags that played Chopin when lit, well – all these thoughts drifted through my head as I listened to waves breaking on a deserted English shore.

The Editor of the *Yorkshire Post* did say this article should be 'funny' – he's barmy! What's funny about sitting in a lonely OP waiting for Germans to come and kill you. Ah! but wait. My friend Gunner Edgington is on the HQ telephone exchange and a drunken Captain Martin is at this moment talking lecherously to his wife in London. So that the conversation isn't wasted he plugs in every OP along the South Coast, bringing a warming glow into a lonely Gunner's life.

Midnight.

'All right, I'm coming.' 'Tis the approaching voice of my seasonal relief – Gunner Chalky White. I stumble back in the dark towards the Fisherman's Cottage, over rubble strewn ground. I'll cut the story short. Two hours later I'm in Hastings General Hospital.

'What a time to break a leg,' says the Casualty Nurse.

'Merry Christmas,' I groaned. Two thousand years ago at this time, Jesus is two hours old and asleep. I wish I was.

Woy Woy

Good God! (Reuter) Am I seeing things? (Milligan) John Fairfax & Sons (Australia) Limited, registered as an oil tanker in Liberia, want *me*, yes *me!*, to write 500 words because I'm a (wait for it) 'well-known Australian'! I don't believe it! Well-known Woy Woyian yes, but Australian? Fairfax can't be fooling, he's enclosed his cheque for $1.90! I rushed to the Commonwealth Savings Bank, Station Road, Woy Woy to cash it.

'We can manage the one dollar,' said the Manager. 'Can you take the rest in stamps?'

Ah, Woy Woy, timeless she lies dreaming in the sun. You can tell when the Pacific Highway goes through Woy Woy – it's cobbled. I remember my first visit. There was only one train a day; it arrived at Woy Woy dead at five o'clock . . . mind you it was just as dead at six o'clock, seven, eight . . . I said to the taxi driver, 'Any night life around here?'

'Yes' he said, hitching up the horse. He took me to a mosquito swamp.

Seriously, I remember Woy Woy before time caught up with her. There was a saying: 'Are you married or do you live in Woy Woy?' It was 1954. My parents had bought a little fibro house in Orange Grove Road called Dunrobbin! A dirt road ran in front and the view then was the Brisbane Waters (only Woy Woy Councillors would name their waters after a city in Queensland). I awoke that first dawn at 5.30 a.m. The sun rose out of the Eastern Pacific. Pied crows, soldier birds and Kookaburras greeted it – there was a golden peace on the land as on the hushed morning waters floated a few insomniac

57

fishermen, hypnotised by their bobbing floats. Off old Mr Jones's wooden pier, sitting immobile, is my brother Desmond on leave from the *Sydney Morning Herald*. He is after that most elusive of seaborn creatures, the black fish. It is a cool crisp morning, dew-hung spiders' webs bounce on the lemon trees.

'Any luck?' I shout to Desmond. He holds up one finger. An hour later three black fish are sizzling in the pan for breakfast.

My Dad, Mam, brother and I sit on the verandah, the golden morning sun warming what could only be an Australian day. The Postie's whistle blows. He's on his bike, followed by a dog – a black mongrel. To this day no one knows who he belonged to. He would join the Postie at the start of his round all the way to Blackwall Mountain, then leave. He did this for six years, then disappeared.

What to do? It's eight o'clock – there's a day ahead. Des and I borrow Wally Tanner's boat. We row across to Daley's Point against the morning tide and are pleasantly surprised by the appearance of a line of porpoise snorting through their blow holes as they surface in the Rip. We row up Cockle Creek beach, tie up, walk up the slope across Daley's Avenue, then up the rocky escarpment. Where, oh where, are those Milligan boys going? To the Aborigine cave, folks! with its flat rock bearing a score of pecked carvings.

In 1954 only a few old locals like Mr Swancott knew of the carvings' existence. Professor McCarthy of Sydney Museum told me it was the haunt of the Dharug or Darug tribe. (He was wrong, it was the Gurangai.) We reached the top and walked along what was left of the Abo trail. Soon we arrived at the great expanse of flat Hawkesbury Sandstone rock, all alive with carvings. A whale shark, a stingray, two corroboree dancers in head dresses, wallaby, barramundi and scores more. Under the lip of the rock was their cave, with kitchen middens three feet deep, 500 years?

Up here there was a great silence, but it was alive with the ghosts of the tribe – there were the children playing, the women pounding roots, the men skinning a roo, others returned with oysters, cockles. They were the first Australians. Now this tribe was extinct. My brother and I stood there in silence. It was New Year's Eve, but only for us – 'they' were in the dreaming time forever.

A survivor from the London Philarmonic Orchestra.

The cast of 'Phantom of the Opera'
as performed by the Scunthorpe Operatic Society.

There's a Lot of it About

Radio Times, famous newspaper, founded by Tom Wireless. This unique paper has asked me to write 800 words – lick, knee, toss, cabbage, pencil, Africa, tool, cupboard, hat-stand (counts as two words), Schnorrer (Jewish, counts as one word, but to you three), twisted, Bazolikon (own word), collect £200 don't pass 'Go', Go directly to Jail, Churchill. There's 20 words to be going on with. Now some bonus words. Vera Lynn (778 to go).

Basically I am supposed to be plugging my television show, 'There's a Lot of it About'. I don't know why, it's not leaking.

So, till that show is televised, here is a game that people can play rather than watching 'Coronation Street'. It's how your Granny can break the world record long jump.

First, dress her in athletic shorts and vest, and spiked running shoes. Bearing in mind the world record long jump is 28 feet, it would be reasonable to assume that she would have to jump at least 28′1″. It's good for her to know these figures beforehand. Now it's possible to exceed this world record by a considerable amount by jumping off a cliff. Pat O'Brien shattered the world record long jump (480 feet) by leaping off Beachy Head. He was awarded the record posthumously. He is now in the *Guinness Book of Records,* as a book marker. So, look forward to seeing you and Granny on Beachy Head.

Now, back to the world record attempt, and while you are going back to the world record attempt, I will continue to write this article.

Did you know that the late Harry Secombe wears ladies' black silk underwear? If you did, tell me *how* did you find out. They say he has a viewing panel in the back of his trousers. It's on a time lock, so you have to be there at the right time to raise the tail of his shirt, allowing you to peer in. If, however, at that moment you find somebody peering out, this means he's taking lodgers.

Incidentally, this show 'There's a Lot of it About' started life on radio as ITMA. With the death of Tommy Hanley, as you know, ITMA broke down. It has been in a garage in Greenwich until now, where I bought it from the Rev. Patrick Tool, Priest and Used Car Dealer.

He assured me, 'I'll tell you this, it's the only four-wheeled ITMA in the country. It looks a bit dodgey now, all you need is a respray.'

Sure enough, as soon as I had a respray to match the car, I found that my whole attitude towards comedy was changed. I thought if I spent enough money on ITMA, have a Turbo installed, it could be even faster and funnier than before, so I went to my Bank Manager.

I said, 'I would like an overdraft of one million pounds.'

He said, 'Don't be a fool, Milligan, put that gun down.'

CHAPTER II

The Hunchback of Notre Dame, now that name rings a bell. It's not very well known that there is also a Hunchback of Notre Catford, and there's even a Hunchback of the late Notre Maurice Chevalier.

I have no idea why they call him the late Maurice Chevalier. As far as I know he was very punctual. I never knew him, and strangely he never knew me; even stranger we never knew each other. It is known that his mother was of Greek descent. She came down in a marble parachute.

No, seriously folks, this is all getting us nowhere. I must now refer to type (a) bureaucrat *Radio Times* type-writing.

The show 'There's a Lot of it About' was forced on me by John Howard Davies, Head of Comedy (also body and legs), who was sitting in his office one day, sipping oxygen through a straw. As he was thumbing through old copies of the *Radio Times,* he came across a death notice that went like this:

The male version of
'Three Little Girls from School are we'.

In Memory of Spike Milligan, Peter Sellers, Harry Secombe and Michael Bentine, who all died in Lower Regent Street, in the BBC Gas Chamber.

He noticed that the spelling of Spike Milligan, was Spike Milla*gna*, and he thought, therefore, that there was just a chance he might still be alive! So, they sent Dynarod to search the building and they reported back to John Howard Davies that Spike Milligan, though 'in a certain condition', that is, he was covered in it, was alive and well and living in terror.

Now, John Howard Davies is not a hard man. He sent a telegram saying: 'All is forgiven come home, bring money.' So, with a lump in my throat, two lumps in my legs, and a horning plastic collar, I came back to that great semi-circular BBC TV Palace, known as 'there it is', and was laid out on John Howard Davies' marble table.

Using 3-in-1, I was massaged back to life with the aid of Neil 'Screws' Shand, Andrew 'Feel' Marshall, and David 'Overdraft' Renwick, to direct the show. A man called Alan Bell was darted and immunised, and was threatened with money unless he produced the show. A quick visit to the Finchley Labour Exchange hastily assembled the aging cast, and *voilà*! A television show.

Now, I'm not quite sure what time they will transmit this gem of comedy. Usually it's Channel 2, so late people think it's the test card with jokes. In fact, the last time I was on the Epilogue was getting higher listening figures than me. You have been forewarned. I will now slide this under the Editor's door and wait for the sound of a pistol shot.

The Goon Show

I never dreamed, that distant day in 1950 when visiting the late Pat Dixon in his cubby hole, Aeolian Hall, Bond Street, that thirty years later the result of that visit could still be heard on Radio Stations as far apart as the USA and Australia. Of course, I'm referring to the Goon Show.

Last year I was holidaying in a little town called Woy Woy, North of Sydney, Australia. I was in the Gun Room of my parents' home oiling the collection of muskets. With one ear (and one leg), I was listening to the ABC. Suddenly I heard what was unmistakably the voice of one Ned Seagoon saying, 'I am only five foot three because I can't stand heights.' Then Grytpype Thynne saying, 'Yes – I believe you had to stand on a chair to reach puberty.'

And I was so taken by surprise I actually laughed at jokes I had written a quarter of a century ago.

Although I have never ever had any ego trips over the show, for the first time I felt, perhaps I have written something that had, has and will go on giving new generations a lot of laughter – and fun. I added up the years and realised that it was perhaps along with 'Take It From Here', the longest running comedy show ever.

It was 4 May 1951 in a little studio off Piccadilly, and today 4 May 1982, BBC4 tell me they are to repeat them yet again – thirty-one years to the day. (I passed this information on to the *Guinness Book of Records* who seemed totally unimpressed.)

Just to verify to myself, I collected my four children, ages 15, 23, 26 and 30, and played them one of the tapes. Their reaction was so

Winston Churchill in drag.

good I realised that the shows hadn't dated. I suppose the real success of the show was in the chemistry of Bentine, Sellers, Secombe – it was like a cannon loaded and primed, all you had to do was light the fuse. One sadness is that all the run-throughs were never recorded, because the ad-libbing and outbursts of genuine hysterical laughter were so contagious.

There was an occasion when Sellers was in mid run-through – accosted by a very thick fireman. There followed a duologue in which Sellers convinced the fireman he was not smoking – the cigarette was a chemical one recommended by the Doctor to cure 'Krollick' from which he suffered. No! the cigarette was not alight – what he was exhaling was not smoke but a 'Krollick' mist being discharged from his affected lungs. The glow on the end of the cigarette was a chemical luminosity caused by the Jell of the chemical components inside the herbal tobacco.

The fireman partially believed it, saying, 'You must think I'm daft.'

Sellers said, 'Of course you're daft – who else would take such a job?' There were nearly fisticuffs – what a pity it was never recorded.

There were also lengthy ad-libs, many in questionable taste, e.g. when Sellers suddenly said, 'Stop the show it's time to auction Bill Greenslade's bum.' In no time bids were coming in, even from the audience. It was all lost in the editing.

The Sunday rehearsals were, for the cast, a form of therapy. The week of appearing in the provinces in variety – with appalling pit orchestras – dull audiences, who only laughed at basic humour – was all shed in comic flights of fancy.

I realise now that the like of it can never happen again. I've been writing comedy for television but without the inspired performances of Bentine, Sellers, Secombe, I've never reached that level of success. Still it did happen; sometimes I wonder if it really did.

A delicate moment in the life of Jack Screws.

John Paul II

Hallelujah! I was so delighted with the Pope's visit that I, in a burst of Irish Catholicism, the intensity of which would have melted St Patrick's crosier, sent a postcard off to the *Catholic Herald* saying how I felt about John Paul's visit here.

They are so elated by the fact that somebody has written to them, they have commissioned me to write 700 words. Well, that's knocked off about fifty, ha! ha! Writing 700 words about John Paul's visit is like describing World War II on the back of a postage stamp.

However, briefly, I am what they call a lapsed Catholic. In fact, I have been lapped by everybody. However, somehow, the Religion seems to stick, and I suppose emotionally I want to stay one so that I may recall those delightful early Church days, the excitement of getting dressed up for my first Communion, the white ribbon round my arm, the special imitation Connemara Marble cover of my Prayer Book, and the lace-edged holy pictures, made in Belgium, and the aluminium holy medals that I wore around my neck, and my scapula. All these memories I want to retain, and the best way is to remain in the Religion that my Mother and Father introduced me to (plus 100 sweating frenzied Nuns).

Going even further back, it must have been a direct line from my predecessors in Ireland who took the Faith some 1,400 years ago. Though I don't go to Church that often I am most certainly indebted to the teachings of Jesus Christ for the way I try to live my life. I try

69

to walk in his footsteps but he seems to have taken giant strides compared to mine.

Nevertheless the incredible durability of the man has lasted down the years, and touched me even in this distant time.

All these feelings, reactions, emotions, distant prayers, the smell of incense, the communion bell, the hand-pumped organs, the Tridentine Mass (which I still prefer) seemed permanently locked inside me, and I was almost beginning to believe that those feelings might be dead, except! switching on the box, this man in white, with good things in him, and with kindly smiling eyes seems to have stirred up my Roman Catholic mess of pottage, and made it taste very acceptable all over again.

I don't think crying is a particularly great emotion. I find tears negative, but I recall the last time I cried over a human was when a friend of mine was killed in Africa, not far from the site where St Cyprian was executed, but seeing this John Paul chap walking among the old and the young, and giving them all a timeless moment of such happiness it seemed to turn the day into Christmas morning. Where I had almost lost faith in the young people of today, only ever reading of them as tattooed yobs, at football matches, beer swilling and throwing bottles, or mugging people in the streets, rioting, beating up innocent people, suddenly I saw a whole arena packed with young people, all as beautiful as the sun, and made even brighter by the presence of this John Paul bloke.

I didn't know how far up the ladder of world importance he was, that is to say, he didn't have flashing lights, amplifiers, he didn't have punk rock purple hair, nor did he yell and shout and jump up and down. In fact, he literally did very little that would get him into the Top Ten. But, the magic of it was he just seemed to turn you on by standing still. Wow! and when I saw the crippled girl of thirteen, in a wheelchair, being touched by him, and watching her face light up with an expression that will remain indelible for me, I was so moved, I cried. That moment said it all, and it all came out like this, L-O-V-E, I just didn't know that there was that much about.

Thank you, John Paul. If there are any errands you want run, or your bicycle tyres pumped up – call me.

The Camel Boy

Once upon a time, in a little Scottish village called Haggis-town lived an old looney Granny. She used to sit in the front room with her feet in a bowl of custard and play the trombone. Her name was Flora – or Ma Gerine! But this story is nothing to do with her – no, this story takes place in the sandy deserts of the Sahara.

In the desert live several tribes of Arabs. One tribe was called the Riffs, their leader was Sheik Arleg. This tribe pitched their tents at the sweet water Oasis of Squirt. Among the tribe was a Mummy and Daddy and a little boy called Hussein, who was seven. They had two camels, a daddy camel called Ras – he had two humps – and a mummy camel called Fakri, who had one hump. The camels used to carry dates and Fairy Liquid to the market in Souk-el-Arba, a big market town in the desert. Hussein's job was to feed and water the camels, keep them nice and clean, and sing pop songs to them. Of all the camel boys at the Oasis he kept his camels the cleanest, because he washed them in Fairy Liquid. Both his camels were lovely and white and they smelt very nice because he used to sprinkle them with Henry Cooper's aftershave lotion. Hussein loved his camels and they loved him.

One evening Hussein led Ras and Fakri to the Oasis for a swim and a drink and a dance. When he got there, he saw another camel boy, called Abdul, hitting an old camel who looked very ill.

'Stop being so cruel,' shouted Hussein. 'Can't you see the camel is ill? He should be in hospital in bed.'

Abdul just laughed. 'Shut up you,' he said. 'He's my camel, I can

71

A premium bond winner with her late husband.

do what I like with him,' and went on beating him.

Hussein was smaller than Abdul, but he rushed at him and tried to stop him. However, Abdul pushed him to the ground and started to beat him. Poor Hussein was getting a terrible beating when suddenly Ras, the daddy camel, grabbed Abdul with his teeth catching hold of him by his bottom.

'Helpppp,' yelled Abdul, as Ras lifted him in the air, then dropped him – Splash! – into the water. Ras kept picking him up and dunking him under the water.

'Stop him,' yelled Abdul.

'Only if you promise not to beat your camel,' said Hussein.

'All right – I promise,' shouted Abdul. Ras let him go and Abdul ran away shouting, 'I'll get my own back on you one day – you see.'

A long way away in Haggis-town, Ma Gerine was still playing her trombone – but . . .

That night, while everyone was asleep, Abdul put poison in the camels' food. Next morning when Hussein went to feed the camels he saw that Ras, the big daddy camel, was dying. All through the day they tried to save him, but that evening he died with all four legs up in the air. All the family were so sad. They buried Ras just outside the date palms. Hussein told his father he thought that Abdul had poisoned Ras with Kentucky Fried Chicken – but his father said, 'Unless we have proof there's nothing we can do.'

A week later Hussein went to take Fakri for a drink. He saw she had a baby boy camel, and, so strange! whereas his daddy used to have two humps and his mammy one, the baby had three – three humps! Exactly the same number of lumps he had in his tea. Hussein was delighted! But to his sorrow, Hussein's Daddy said, 'My boy, I'm sorry to tell you that three-humped camels are bad luck. If you keep it, your pussy cat's legs will fall off. There is an old Chinese proverb:

'A camel with three humps
Will put the family in the dumps.'

Dick Scratcher before the operation with his dog Hercules. Catford 1932.

'We'll have to kill him,' said Father.

Hussein was horrified. 'Kill him? Why? Why can't we sell him?'

'Because no one will buy a dead three-humped camel – they won't even buy a live one!'

Hussein begged and pleaded, and offered to let him have his Action

Dick, now Rita, Scratcher after the operation. The dog Hercules (now Priscilla) also had the operation. Catford 1933.

Man, but his Father said, 'No, tomorrow at dawn I will have to shoot him.'

That night, Hussein waited until everyone was asleep, and going zzzz, then packing up his belongings he crept out and, taking the baby camel, he ran off into the desert. All night he wandered – it was cold – then, in the distance, he saw firelight coming from a cave. As he got nearer he saw it was an old Arab with a long beard, making coffee, and watching 'Koranation Street' on his old leather TV set.

Hussein came near and said, 'Excuse me, Sir, we are very cold. Can we sit by your fire?'

The old man smiled, 'By Allah! a little boy and a baby camel – yes, come in – here have some fishes' fingers and chips.'

Hussein ate the food. He told the old man what had happened.

The old man laughed. 'Don't believe that silly tale about three-humped camels. You can, if you like, work for me.'

The old man was Sheik Bourgiba, a famous trainer of racing camels and cats. He was in the desert looking for young camels to train for racing.

A long way away in the little . . .

'Oh dear,' he said. 'That camel has had a close shave.' Hussein didn't understand. He didn't know that camels shaved, but he remembered he had never seen a camel with a long beard, so perhaps Sheik Bourgiba was right, perhaps his camel *did* have a close shave.

'Now,' said Sheik Bourgiba. 'You must guard your camel all right. Take this record of Barry Manilow, play it all night – that should keep anybody away.' And that's what Hussein did.

Several years passed by. One day Sheik Bourgiba called Hussein to his tent. 'Boy, I have entered you and Lucky in the Camel Derby at Kairoun. If you win you will be a rich boy: the first prize is twelve pounds of gold, second prize is The Pope.'

The night before the great race, Hussein was so excited he couldn't sleep, so he went down to the stable to see Lucky who was asleep in the straw. Hussein cuddled down next to him and fell asleep.

A sudden noise awakened him and he saw a shadowy figure coming into the stable. The figure bent over the camel's feed bucket and poured something from a bottle.

'Hi you,' yelled Hussein. The figure jumped up and ran away. Hussein picked up the bottle on the floor. It was marked 'Arsenic – Poison. Keep out of reach of adults, children, camels and Mrs Thatcher.' Hussein ran and told Sheik Bourgiba.

Away in a Scottish village called Haggis-town Ma Gerine was

playing her trombone when a tree fell on her.

The morning of the great Camel Derby dawned. At the great racing field at Kairoun, thousands of people were arriving from all over Africa. Among them were Hussein's Mum and Dad who, by now, hadn't seen their son for twelve years, and thought he was dead. But we know he wasn't dead, because dead jockeys aren't allowed to ride camels.

So came the great race. There were camels from all over the world: there was a British Leyland camel, with only three legs; a camel from Japan; the camel from Ireland was a donkey. As the thirty camels lined up for the start, the Sultan on his throne raised his golden sword, pulled the trigger – BANG – and off went the camels in a great cloud of dust. Round and round the race course went the cloud of dust with the camels inside.

Someone who wasn't interested in the race was a Scottish lady in Haggis-town, who was sitting with her feet in a bowl of custard while she played the trombone.

Meantime, inside the cloud of dust, Hussein was in the lead.

'Only one more lap, Lucky, and we've won,' he said. Just then he felt a blow on his neck. Looking round, he saw the jockey behind him on a black camel lunge at Hussein with his whip. It was, was it? Yes – Abdul, the cruel boy from Squirt Oasis!

'Ged up – Lucky – faster, boy,' said Hussein, at the same time sticking a pin in Lucky's bum. Whoosh! Lucky shot forward, clear of the crowd of dust and Whoosh! past the winning post – the Winner.

From the stands Hussein's Mum and Dad could hardly believe their eyes. 'It's our son,' they cried. Soon they were all re-united.

Hussein was now rich. He took his Mum, Dad and his camel to dinner at Mrs Dumpling's dining-rooms for refined camels.

A long way away Ma Gerine was playing her trombone when the roof fell in.

77

Eric Balls, a retired plumber's mate, with his dog Nutts. Lewisham 1930.

Muriel Balls, his wife, with Nutts on her lap.

Eric Balls and Family at Virginia Water, 1933.
'We took the tube to Ruislip and then walked –
we left Nutts at home with Molly.'

The Countryman

Yes, I love the British countryside, though my access to it came late, thanks to Adolf Hitler. Let me explain. I was born one torrid afternoon in 1918 at the Cantonment Military Hospital of a British Remount Depot in Ahmednagar, India.

My nascent years were spent in the junglesque atmosphere of a Kipling boyhood. My father was never stationed in any giant metropolis like Bombay, Karachi or Calcutta, but places like Poona, Belgaum, all semi-rural. Being born to the Regiment (The Royal Horse Artillery), at the tender age of four I was riding through the wild Indian countryside. I existed for the out-of-doors. To me, houses were for changing your clothes in, so my boyhood was the countryside with trees like the tamarind, the mango, the bhorum trees. Farmers used wooden ploughs and bullocks; they planted by hand with a piece of sharpened 'luckery'. To me, all cattle were emaciated, and the ringing of goat bells ran through my boyhood. Instead of foxes and badgers, it was monkeys, mongoose, cobras and scorpions. The sun blazed on the parched maidans in summer, and steamed as the monsoon rains deluged the landscape.

Imagine the explosive quality of seeing, at the age of twenty-one, the lush of the English countryside for the first time. It was an experience that bordered on the hallucinogenic. From India I came to live in the black fogbound gloom of London in the depressing 1930s. Then came the 'call to arms' and one golden sunlit day in June 1940 I caught the 9.10 train from Victoria to report to the regiment at Bexhill-on-Sea.

81

Imagine the privilege of living in an English country town on the sea with most of the residents fled, and no *tourists*. The first thing was the air – that *attarent* perfume of ozone and chlorophyll was a heady mixture. So unused to its scent, I kept asking people was there a perfume factory nearby.

What opened up the countryside were the route marches. Marching down a hedgerow-lined country lane was for me an experience that I presume pot smokers must have. For a start I had never seen hedgerow flowers. At every halt ('Fall out for a smoke') I was aware of curious khaki eyes watching Gunner Milligan observing these small wayside miracles. I've no idea what it is in a wayside flower that makes a human being its slave. I bought a large hardbacked book, and started pressing specimens. Not only did these silent miniature plants beckon with their shape, texture and colour, but a new delight – their names:

Bitter-Sweet, Jack-by-the-hedge, Travellers Joy, Dove's-foot Crane-bill.

The list is endless. Driving my Humber Wireless Truck I would move off the main roads and take secondary routes at a steady 15 m.p.h. I drove through the apple orchards and took in the overpowering perfume of apple blossom in full spate on a warm May evening. I didn't know that England could smell as exquisite as the jasmine nights of Elephanta Island.

Hard-hit Sussex farmers (whose workers were sitting in trenches in Libya) called for help with the harvest; standing on one of those magnificent Sussex farm wagons (now almost extinct) with a pitch fork, bailing hay, I felt like God. I had become so emotionally integrated with the country that even the farm implements were exciting. I wondered at the elegance of those two slender slightly curving steel horns of the hay fork, not only its aesthetic quality but it was the *perfect* manual tool for the job.

At that time I was shown my first corn dolly. The farmer's wife told me her mother taught her to make them and showed me how.

Doris Fool and Motts the neutered cat.
Catford 1930.

She said it went back to Anglo-Saxon times and had a religious significance that was possibly Celtic.

Cows. English Cows, dripping with beef and awash with milk, were these the same species as those wretched Indian skeletons? What a sight on a sunlit day to stand on a high point of the Downs and watch a landscape of alarming green bespattered with the red and white of the Herefords and the black and white of the Friesians and the dun of the Jerseys.

This was the English countryside. It sang at you; this was the reason Constable never painted anything else. The pleasures of those years were endless – from seeing a rare Medlar tree to a Saxon dew pond, an unspoilt bluebell-wood at Winchelsea, a working windmill at Hog Hill. Fred Vahey, a Sussex Thatcher, living in a Gipsy caravan, making nettle soup from a Roman recipe – the list of countryside delights was endless.

That was then. Now . . . it's forty-one years later. Alas, our countryside, I stress *OUR* countryside, is (a) being eroded, (b) mutilated, (c) cruel farming methods are being evolved.

When you realise that *3,800* hedgerows have vanished since the war and the process has not been halted, the future looks bleak. 'Prairie' farming is one villain, factory farming the other. As one of those who is horrified by the dramatic changes in countryside husbandry I, needless to say, joined every conservation group there was. I was soon embroiled with people who were genuinely concerned. But, being concerned, joining the RSPCA, writing to *The Times* etc, is all very well, but these very people who point fingers at the factory farmer and say 'Farming Battery chickens is cruelty' should look to the *real* offender – *the people who buy battery chicken eggs.*

Farmers did not dream up intensive farming. No, it was the pressure of greater demand at cheaper prices, so that families to whom chicken was a luxury could have one whenever they wanted. *This applies to the cruelty in the brief lives of veal calves, etc.* Factory Farmer Giles is only obeying the demands for more and cheaper food. *The niggers in the woodpile are* you *and* me.

I asked one lady who was outraged by it all, 'Do you eat meat?' She said, 'Yes.' Now this woman was a tireless worker for animal rights. I said if you object to battery farming, how can you support the slaughter of millions of cows, etc, every day. She said, 'It's not as cruel as factory farming.' I told her a visit to an abattoir in full spate might change her mind.

So, what is killing the countryside is pressure from increasing *population* and *affluence*; depression or not people still have more money than of yore, and there are *more* of us than of yore. The result is tremendous pressure on land and the fruits of the land. The only way to reverse this physical and moral erosion is first to *stabilise* our numbers and then in controlled and humane circumstances *reduce* our numbers; when you think that in 1830 we were only 11,000,000 in number and animals on farms lived in happy natural conditions, our hedgerows flourished, our arable fields were of human proportion. Not like the insane Canadian and American limitless acres that reach from the horizon with no tree or hedge to break the monotony. All the results of massive population demand.

There was a time when the countryside could tolerate the traffic of tourists, now the increase in numbers has, for the first time in our history, caused progressive erosion that forces authorities to close areas down to allow them to recover (Snowdonia), yet despite this writing on the wall no one takes direct population control measures – least of all the Government. China (too late) has realised the numbers disaster they have on their doorstep (*two billion*) and have introduced restrictions on people having more than two children, but they are the only ones.

If we are to save our delightful countryside, there is only one way. Malthus was right, if you want the countryside to survive – small families please, preferably vegetarians.

The dog Nutts has run away from Eric Balls and lives with Scottish soldiers. Bottom right – Private McHares is pointing to two other dogs, Mac and Scottie.

Air Travel

It's no good. I can't stand it any more! No more old fashioned GWR trains with Rococo carriages – no more Brighton Belle with Sir Laurence Olivier reading *The Stage,* with a brandy. I am suffering Victorian-type-Travel withdrawal symptoms. I have to travel by air – yes – but, my God, I yearn for my Victorian past, those long gone travelling days in India, the Bullock cart – Tonga – Rickshaw – Victoriana – and across India in steam trains with Victorian Raj interiors – dining-cars all red plush, polished brass, turbanned GIP bearers, likewise P&O Liners, The *Kaiser Hinde,* teak panelling, dining saloon, sanded decks, polished decks.

I write this as an appeal to the airlines of the world for a Victorian gas-lit airliner – yes, let it be jet, but I suggest the following nostalgia modifications: uniforms, of course, air hostesses will wear crinolines and bustles, the stewards will wear the full uniform of the Naval Petty Officers of 1900. The crew will wear the uniform of the 17th Lancers, or the Grenadier Guards of 1887. After passing over Italy they will change to tropical whites. The interior of the planes will be wallpapered in William Morris style, all seats will be buttoned velvet, with brass fittings, windows will be porthole shaped, brass bound, with floral damask curtains and black canvas blinds.

Between the pilot and co-pilot must be placed a roaring coal fire. Oil paintings by Landseer should be tastefully arranged around the walls of the entire plane. In the 'Hump' on the 747 must be all Royal Scarlet Velvet, and a marble floor. Potted palms tastefully arranged in Jardinières. Music will be provided, a trio – violin, cello and harp –

in evening dress. That's First Class. The Peasants in Economy will have a Gypsy Trio, plus a conjurer. Ice buckets will be attached to all seats – all containing wine of the traveller's choice. Nothing less than Première Cru for First Class.

At the rear of the plane – broadside – will be a Pub Bar, with barrelled real *ale* on draught. The music on take off will be 'Land of Hope and Glory', on landing 'God Save the Queen'. The crew will at no time broadcast those noisy messages such as 'We are passing over Naples, Birmingham etc, etc.' They will remain silent – servile – and do naught but *GROVEL* to the passengers unless called upon to sing the resident comic song that goes 'Hello hello, we're sorry we're late, we apologise for the delay, etc, etc.'

Gratuities: when passengers debouch, the cockpit and cabin crew will dress the landing steps and salute and call for three cheers for the passengers. The Captain will solicit gratuities by holding out his hat, and saying 'God bless you Sir – remember an old airline pilot – Good luck. Travel with us again. Please – we're skint.'

So there – Milligan points to a new age in Air Travel – I await the first gas-lit flight.

Mr Lonely

Who is Sid Lewis? Who is Mr Lonely? Both are one and the same person, both a figment of Eric Morecambe's imagination, which has materialised with the name Mr Lonely. When I read it, at first I was under the illusion that Sid Lewis was a real person – after all, wasn't he there on a photograph on the cover? – likewise photos of Sid Lewis on his wedding day with Eric Morecambe in attendance? More convincing still, a guitar solo 'Mr Lonely' written by Sid Lewis. Yet, for all my twenty-seven years in showbiz (yes twenty-seven, no knighthood, no Variety Club dinner – nothing!!!) I could not recall any Sid Lewis. Sid James, Vic Lewis, Sid Fields, Vic Oliver, Sid Seymour, yes – but Sid Lewis? No alas, there is no Sid Lewis. But, and here we start lauding Eric Morecambe's knowledge and experience of the profession, as the pages turn Sid Lewis becomes a reality.

I could call Eric the Samuel Pepys of the stand-up comics, for the simple prose of Morecambe is so ideal in describing the day by day (in some cases minute by minute) life of this man that I would say it was the first time we've had a book, written of a showbiz character, by a showbiz character, in showbiz jargon. Its basic success lies in its simplicity, yet a simplicity with a magnificent eye for the plastic details of the entertainment world. It is remarkable that despite Eric having scaled the peaks of his profession he never once painted the profession as glamorous – he takes off the façade and shows the raw flesh – the guts – the smelly back stage, ashtrays with dog ends – jock straps on washing lines, the empty glossy front.

Eric's recollection of those comedy routines, fashioned for late night drunk audiences, that deep down every comic with any real talent loathes. For Sid Lewis's routine on some tourist-trap nightclub, the standard answer to barrackers: 'You're lousy – get off.'

'Ah, it's the man from rent-a-mouth.'

'Good evening ladies and gentlemen it's really great to be here etc. etc.'

To a married couple: 'That your husband or has the waiter been sick?'

As I write, thousands of stand-up comics are doing the same routine. This book is the very best example I've read which describes a profession that is looked on, by all except those in it, as glamorous. It is bitter-sweet, and so unlike anything I thought Eric Morecambe would have written – of course it means more to myself and fellow comics who have lived through the dying era of music hall, and the end-of-the-pier shows.

The story of Sid Lewis or anyone like him will not come again. He is a product of post-World War II – a species like myself, Harry Secombe, Eric and Ernie, Tommy Cooper etc. Secombe writes of it, equally successfully in *Twice Brightly,* but you have to have lived it to have written it, unlike John Osborne's *The Entertainer* – very good, but lacking that essential ingredient, personal experience.

I would like to give quotes from the book, but it would spoil the reader's enjoyment. I found the book a little jewel – it had the *real* showbiz ending. A sad one. Well done Eric.

Molly, who was looking forward to her trip on the Titanic.

'If you don't know which one is me you should'
– Len, Tom and Len – Glasgow 1901.
(Tom is the other one.)

Richard Henry Sellers
(known as Peter Sellers)

Born 8 September, 1925. Died, London, 24 July, 1980.

Peter's mother was a Jewess who married out of the religion to William Sellers. Not many people know that through his mother's side of the family he is a direct descendant of Daniel Mendoza, who once taught George IV. He was primarily educated at St Aloysius College in Hornsey Lane, and an RC school run by the Brothers of Our Lady of Mercy.

His introduction to the entertainment world was via his mother, who was one of the Ray Sisters, and his father who was a pianist of modest ability.

He did most jobs backstage, assisting, sweeping up, call boy etc, and eventually was filled with the desire to play drums in a dance band. He became very proficient at this, and, but for his ability at mimicry, he might well have stayed a jazz drummer.

Called up to the RAF during the war, despite his mother's desperate efforts to have him disqualified on medical grounds, he finally ended up in the Entertainment Section of the RAF in India, Ceylon, and Burma with Ralph Reader's Gang Show. Within a short time of leaving the Services in 1947, such was his confidence and his ability as an impressionist, he duped a BBC Producer, by using the voice of Kenneth Horne. The Producer was duly impressed, and gave him a small part in a comedy show.

In a short space of time he had appeared in the following series: Petticoat Lane, Ray's a Laugh, Variety Bandbox, Workers' Playtime, Third Division (the first comedy show to come on the erudite Third Programme), finally reaching the highest acclaim in the revolutionary Goon Show.

During this period he also appeared in Variety, including the Royal Command Performance. There were a few second-rate films: *Penny Points to Paradise* (1951), *Orders are Orders* (1954), *John and Julie* (1955), *The Smallest Show on Earth* (1957), and a strangely original short film written and directed by Spike Milligan, entitled *The Running Jumping Standing Still Film*. It won numerous awards because of its innovatory ideas.

His big commercial break came in *The Lady Killers* (1955) and he received world acclaim for his stunning performance in *I'm All Right, Jack* (1959). There followed a series of quality films, some successful, some not, including playing opposite Sophia Loren in *The Millionairess* (1961), and *Waltz of the Toreadors* (1962), and one produced and directed by himself, *Mister Topaze* (1961).

He did a number of black comedy films, one being *What's New, Pussycat?* (1965), with Peter O'Toole and Woody Allen.

Then came the watershed in his career, his portrayal of Inspector Clouseau, in *The Pink Panther* (1963). There followed a period of indifference, and it would appear at one time that his career might have come to a conclusion. However, there followed *The Return of the Pink Panther* (1974) and *The Pink Panther Strikes Again* (1976), which renovated his career and made him a millionaire.

Alas, he suffered with a heart condition in the last fifteen years of his life, which made life difficult for him, and had a debilitating effect on his personality.

None of his marriages was successful in terms of durability. His first one to Anne Hayes produced two children, Michael and Sarah. This marriage was terminated, and in a whirlwind romance, he married starlet, Britt Ekland. There was one child from this marriage, Victoria. The marriage was dissolved, and he married Miranda Quarry, with no more success than previously. His last marriage to Lynne Frederick also underwent emotional undulations, and even

94

though they remained married until the day he died, all the signs point to a marriage that had failed.

To summarise him, one would say that he was one of the most glittering comic talents of our age, but what few people know is he never reached or was allowed to perform the levels of comedy that he delighted in most, this being the nonsense school. To his dying day he said his happiest days were performing in the Goon Shows.

He made a desperate attempt to recreate the Goon Show atmosphere by making the film *The Fiendish Plot of Dr Fu Manchu* (1980), which he co-wrote. Alas he never ever was a writer, or ever would be, and collaborating with Americans, who had no like sense of humour, the film was a failure.

However, almost miraculously, he gave his finest performance in his last film but one *Being There* (1979). It showed mostly his incredible ability to recreate a character, in which Peter Sellers himself seemed to be totally excluded. In my own humble opinion this man was more than a genius, he was a freak. His last wry contribution to comedy was having Glen Miller's 'In the Mood' played at his cremation.

Peter Sellers
(known as Richard Henry Sellers)

Peter Sellers died a year ago. I miss him – not so much for friendship – but for the humour. The humour that only he, I and a few others could understand. It was a humour that never saw the light of day in any of his pictures; Directors, Producers, writers only saw the *obvious* side of Peter, his brilliant mimicry and his commercial sense of humour. Cinema audiences *never* saw the comedy level that Peter Sellers *wanted* to reveal, only once did we see it in the *Running, Jumping Standing Still Film*.

He and I must have spent thousands of pounds phoning each other, just to relate any 'far out' comic incident that had taken our fancy. I would phone him in France from Woy Woy (where??), Australia. I would make my mother speak first and say to him, 'This is Spike Milligan's mother phoning from Woy Woy.' This invoked paroxysms of laughter from him and I would take over the phone and laugh at him laughing.

When he had recovered he would assume the voice of a Pakistani Bank Manager on a crossed line. The conversation would go:

Sellers: Hello, Hel-lo? What is happening?
Spike: (As idiot Woy Woy Exchange op): Just a minute – I'll put yez thro.
Pakistani Bank Manager: Thro – but I am thro – is Mr Banergee in?
Woy Woy Operator: No this is the Woy Woy Exchange.
Pa Bank Mang: Woy Woy?? What is a Woy Woy?
Woy Woy Op.: It's a telephone exchange.

96

Pa Bank Mang: What is happening – is Mr Banergee there?
Woy Woy Op.: What?
Pa Bank Mang: I was speaking to Mr Banergee and he was cut off –

At this point I would hand the phone to my father and make him
speak.

Father: Hello – this is Spike Milligan's father speaking.

Sellers would maintain his character.

Pa Bank Mang: I don't wishing to speak to Spike Milligan's father –
I want to speak to Mr Banergee.

My father – who was unaware of the joke – said to me, 'This isn't
Peter Sellers – it's a wog asking for Mr Banergee.'
    If no one thinks it funny – good – we had it all to ourselves.
    The best one we ever did was when we were on tour in Variety. We
were both visually unknown (*Radio* Stars); we kept all our props in
a large wicker basket. We were to stay at theatrical digs, Hagley
Road, Birmingham. I arrived at the door with the wicker basket. Mrs
Reeves opened the door. 'Ah yes, you've booked for the week.' I
struggled to pull the heavy basket up the stairs – she got her son and
her husband. 'It's very heavy – what you got in it?'
    We finally got it into my bedroom. When I opened the basket
Sellers steps out and says, 'Thank you – it's my legs you know.'
    Another time we recorded a series of heavy straining – backed by
piano music by Chopin, much like someone in the loo having a bad
time. We knew a very proper couple – real square – who could talk
on any serious subject, but who had no sense of humour.
    We invited them to dinner. Sellers said, 'I've got a tape of the new
Music Concerto by Le Roté.' Through dinner the straining continued.
Comments from our guests: 'Very original'; 'I like the music'; 'Who
is he?' The comment that broke us up was, 'Is it the pianist straining?' –
to which Sellers said, 'Yes – he's got the shits.' They never came
again.

Len Leggs, Eric's neighbour, going in a direction.
Deptford.

We got on a bus. The conductor arrives. 'Fares please,' he says. Sellers turns to me and says, 'Where are we going?' From a cardboard box I produce a telephone and proceed to dial. I speak in a Prussian accent.

'Hello, is zat zer German Embassy? – Vere are we going?' I turned and informed Herr Sellers: 'Düsseldorf.'

Peter passed this on to the conductor who told us the bus only went as far as Wood Green. We would jump to our feet and rush off the vehicle saying, 'It's zer wrong bus – hurry, we'll miss dinner.'

This article springs from my knowledge of Peter, but I stress it because, whereas many others have written biographies, articles, stories, they were all the result of research, interviews. I don't need any research – I speak from direct contact – for instance once when

Len Leggs on a different bike going in a different direction.
New Cross.

he invited Prince Charles, Secombe and myself to lunch at Elstead. To this day *no one* knows that we planned that throughout the meal Prince Charles and his ADC Squadron Leader Checketts would get smaller portions than any one else. I had six potatoes on my plate, Charles four, his steak was two ounces lighter, four sprouts less than the others. Every now and then I would catch Peter's eye and the effort to contain our laughter was a major effort.

Why did we do it? Insanity. Another time I phoned him in LA. I put the call through the operator. I put on a very old weak man's voice and asked the operator if he could pass my weak-voiced message on to Mr Sellers. He agreed. Peter answered.

Me (very weak): Hello, son – it's your Uncle Plaques.

Peter: Who?
Operator: Hello, son – it's your Uncle Plaques.
Peter: Hello, Uncle – how are your varicose veins?
Me: What?
Operator: He says how are your varicose veins.
Me: I had the operation on Saturday – Dr Reuben Croucher did it.
Operator: Did you get that?
Peter: Yes – Uncle.
Me: What?
Peter: Tell Aunty I'm sending the chimpanzee by sea mail.
Me: What?
Operator: He's sending your Aunty the chimpanzee by sea mail.

The unsuspecting operator continued to pass on details of operations, a fatal hernia, a mongrel that preferred bird seed, etc, etc.

In the early days, when Peter lived over a flower shop in Finchley, I was broke. He was earning £50 a week – rich! rich! rich! We were together constantly (this was before the Goon Show) and all those hours were spent exploring comedy at a lunatic level – I don't mean slapstick – but forcing a logical situation to appear insane – i.e. we had an audition – it's unlike any theatrical audition since the applicants are high court judges and the auditioners are criminals.

Criminal: Next please.
(*Enter a Judge.*)
Judge: For my first sentence I'd like to do Jalum *v* the Crown. I
    sentence you to six years' hard labour.
Criminal: Next!
2nd Judge: I'd like to do the case of Gun Thru the child molester.
    There's far too much of this sort of thing ...
Criminal: Next please!

The idea behind it was the loss of confidence in the Judicial system whose variation in imposing sentences suggest they made the law up themselves. A man would murder a child and get three months; another man would ill-treat a dog and get six. So behind the humour was a searching for truth. As to Peter himself, he was devil and angel. He did wonderful things, he did terrible things. I'll remember him for his wonderful things.

Rugby

'Write a thousand words on something about Rugby,' says David Norrie of Dragon's Delight, 'preferably about Gareth Edwards.'

My God, how can you say *anything* about Edwards in a thousand words, even one hundred thousand. It would take all of that to describe his epic chip-ahead try against Scotland.

I remember jumping up and shouting, 'There is a God, they should build a Chapel there.' To my undying shame I only watched it on TV, but it had its rewards. As Gareth got up the camera gave a close-up and he said something (I think to Mervyn Davis). With the aid of Cliff Morgan and his grapevine, I discovered the first words Gareth said after the try were 'Bloody long way.'

No, I can't cover him in one thousand words, but it will suffice for brief coverage of a game I played in December 1944. The place Sparinise in Italy.

It started when I joined the Royal Artillery in 1939. I was seized by a thick-set chunky Welshman (Pineapple Balls we called him), one Sergeant Lew Griffin who had heard I played Rugby; up 'til then I had played wing three-quarter for the South-East London Polytechnic, a crowd of fifteen spotty lads held together with pimples, fear and hair-oil. Lew Griffin looked like he had been born a lock forward. He was the size of Frank Cotton – had a nose so flattened that even full face it was in profile. The team was 'D' Battery of the 56th Heavy Regiment. It was good fun, we were excused guard duties – time off for training, when training (training? ha, ha, ha) excused morning parades.

But to the game. We were in action around Cassino, when the word came we were to pull out for a rest. The rest consisted of a tent and a muddy field. It was better than nothing – no wait! it wasn't. Lew Griffin decides that a rest should include a few games, and so it came to pass after much argument and threats, we were to play a scratch Infantry Team called The Rest.

'So this is what they call a Rest,' said our hooker, Paddy Main.

Came the day it was so dark we thought it was night. Black clouds with ice-cold showers covered the proceedings with gloom.

'It's too bloody dark to see,' I said.

'Don't worry,' said Griffin. 'We'll play in braille.' He cheered us up with hot tea laced with 90 proof Navy Rum.

We watched as The Rest arrived in a Three Tonner. As they debouched, the front row gasped. They were all over six foot, weighed thirteen to fifteen stone, were smothered in black hair, and with the backs of their hands dragging along the ground. I remember thinking their HQ must have been in a tree.

'I'm not playing them until I hear one of them talk.'

It turns out they are a mixture of Scots' Grenadiers, and Irish Guards (201 Guards Brigade).

The 'pitch' left much to be desired, like a surface. The mud was about 6 inches deep, with puddles of water. As if that wasn't bad enough, it sloped 20 degrees. The referee – Captain B. Smythe, RE – had played for the Wasps.

The toss: Griffin turned to us and said, 'We're playing up the deep end.'

What was to make the game interesting was a drunken Scots Guards piper who started to play the Skye Boat Song when a try was imminent – which in this game was well nigh permanent. I will only describe certain incidents in this game – all the rest was a massacre of the innocents. The sheer weight impetus of the Guardsmen coming down hill towards us was unstoppable – their scrums put on a show that sent the whole thing sliding downhill towards our line. As Paddy Main, our hooker, said, 'It's like being bloody well shunted.' The only thing that stopped us was the mud piling up behind. There was no hold in the ground. I successfully tackled fifteen feet from our

103

Fred Trousers outside his Animal Welfare shop, Peckham, January 1930.
Bankrupt February 1930. He sold Spratts.

Mr Krells, the landlord who broke him.
'I'll have him for every penny he owns.'
— It came to 12 pounds.

line, but the monster just slid me over the line with him.

At 28–0, as Griffin said, they appeared to be winning.

After ten minutes' frantic play, neither side were distinguishable for the mud. Before we could pass we were down to shouting 'Who are you?' Running down the line, about to pass, I shouted 'Gunner?' The reply: 'No, spectator.'

I was about to find out to what ends dedicated Welshmen will go playing Rugby – I was in a maul in the Guardsmen's half, during which I was knocked unconscious. When I came to, I was below ground level in a shallow grave. Hearing voices I looked up to see 'D' Battery in possession and coming this way. At the sight of me getting up, came the anguished voice of Lew Griffin, 'Don't get up!! You'll put us offside.' I lay back as the hoard thundered over me.

'Sorry about that,' said Griffin.

'*You're* sorry,' I said.

Blessed relief – half-time came with the Guardsmen leading 33–0. We were a battered lot. Full back Marsden pointed to a lump on his forehead like an egg.

'Oh yes, boyo,' said Griffin, 'they are a rough lot.'

Marsden moaned. 'It wasn't one of them it was one of us.'

'Now,' said Griffin, 'don't be dispirited. We're not losing, it's just that they've got more points than us.'

'That's because they have got an extra man.'

'Who?' I said.

'That bloody referee!!'

'Let's tackle him then,' said Tiny Vicars.

Griffin gave his Backs-to-the-Wall orders. 'Now listen, they don't like going back.'

''Ow do you know,' says Gunner Leech. 'They haven't gone back yet.'

'They're Irish, they don't know the way back.'

'We've lost every strike against the head.'

'I know,' says Griffin. 'From now on, risk it, don't put it in straight.'

'I haven't been putting in straight,' moaned scrum half.

He summarised: 'We've lost every set piece.'

I interrupted. 'The way we're playing we've even lost the bloody interval.'

Griffin is resolute – he pokes me in the chest with an obstetrical finger. 'Milligan, you are the sort of Rugby Player that can snatch defeat out of the jaws of Victory.'

I grinned.

The whistle calls us.

'Remember,' Griffin shouts. 'Plenty of loose ball – lots of up and under, try and avoid set pieces.'

The rain is now obscuring the posts. Visibility is nil – like our score.

'Let's go home,' I said. 'They won't miss us.'

We kick off – brilliant, straight into touch. What a team, as our Captain said. We had the will to lose. Rain – Rain. I could hear one hooker praying for death in the scrum.

The up and unders paid off. The Guards, looking up to see the ball, mouths opened, nearly drowned. The ball was grease, to pass it you didn't throw, you squeezed, and it shot out of your hands like a glycerine suppository from a bottom.

The pitch was like a swimming pool. In these conditions I scored our only try, again an up and under. Their full back (really full – he was pissed) muffed the catch with us all bearing down. I got possession. Ten yards from the line, the full back made a despairing lunge, grabbed my shorts, as I – wait for it – dived *under* the line, to re-appear on the other side *sans* shorts wearing the remains of a jock strap. All this and we lost.

No, friends, Rugby is for watching – not playing.

'Jock' after Swedish Massage – Woy Woy 1928.

On the Couch

Doctor has asked me to write about my experience of Psychiatry. I have a layman's knowledge of medicine – aspirins. But I can speak as a patient with a long history of mental illness, therefore my opinions of Psychiatrists are those of someone 'on the couch'. My historical knowledge tells me that with the coming of Psychiatry we had the last addition of human importance to medicine. Prior to about 1880 a person was either sane or mad; the latter was usually committed to Bedlam or places like it. Even in comparatively 'modern' mental institutions, I have seen that abomination, the padded cell – the invention of desperation and failure. It seems to me that because of its abstract quality, mental illness is one of the most frustrating, sometimes manifesting itself in nurses being violent towards patients (itself a form of neurosis). There certainly is a stage in some mental cases where the medical world is baffled.

I have experience of Psychiatrists actually saying to a patient: 'I can't do any more for you.' The shock to a patient is rather like a surgeon performing a bowel operation then telling the patient, 'I'm sorry I can't sew you up, I've had enough.' When I was a patient at Roehampton Priory, at the back of a book cupboard I came upon a hospital log dating back to 1899. The fact that it had a lock on it shows the degree of secrecy associated with mental illness. There were many entries. I will just repeat one:

EDWINA MORRIS: AGE 49
1915   Depression since loss of Son

1916	No change
1917	No change
1918	No change
1919	No change
1920	No change
1921	No change
1922	No change
1923	No change
1924	No change
1925	No change
1926	No change
1927	No change
1928	Died

Baffling. No cure. Sad. Indeed Psychiatry has a very positive yes–no (ying–yang) quality. It is shot through with miserable failures and miraculous cures, the latter being catatonic patients treated with L-Dopa. One sad observation is the lack of understanding by the public for neurotics even those near and dear. A friend of mine, a manic depressive, is taunted by his wife: 'You're fuckin' mad aren't you.' I have had Psychiatrists, loved ones, sit by my bed, who were miles away emotionally. Out of sight, man.

Believe me love and understanding works more than any drug. The 'hope' of the neurotic is the Psychiatrist, most certainly he goes to him with the hope of a 'cure' – why not? Doctors do it for coughs and colds. Alas, there comes the shock for the neurotic, treatment can go on and on, and I speak from personal experience.

My own case started that distant day, January 1944. I had been wounded, but worse I had what World War I called Shell Shock – now called Battle Fatigue, better diagnosed as Shit Scared. I found myself crying and stammering at a Casualty Clearing Hospital near Cassino. A Captain Psychiatrist sat behind a table. He must have thought me deaf. He shouted: 'YOU WILL GET BETTER, DO YOU UNDERSTAND?' Thirty years have gone, I'm still waiting. His attempt at treating me went like this: 'Don't worry. Do you know it takes 100,000 shells to kill one man?' What a man, I thought. I was sent to a tent, and given some white pills. I slept twenty-four hours, feeling drowsy.

What disturbed me was no diagnosis; what was wrong with me? How long would it last? What was the cure? He wasn't a very good Psychiatrist. I was to meet worse. I was sent to Caserta Military Hospital where I met the formidable Major Palmer, innovator of Deep Narcosis for Battle Fatigue. My interview with him brimmed with intelligence and perception.

PALMER:	What do you think is wrong with you?
MILLIGAN:	I don't know, but I think I've had enough.
PALMER:	Do you want to go back to your Regiment?
MILLIGAN:	Yes, but I don't think it advisable.
PALMER:	Why?
MILLIGAN:	I don't think I'm reliable, I might let my mates down.
PALMER:	How long have you been in the line?
MILLIGAN:	About five months. Since Salerno.

He started to write. 'I agree you've had it, Milligan. I'm recommending you be downgraded to B2.' It was as short and as simple as that. No pills, but already I felt better. I had been given a category that made my illness positive, not spoken down to. What I still did not know was that as far on as 1964, I would still be 'B2'.

I returned to civilian life as an Anxiety State Chronic. The pressure of the entertainment world soon saw me going into a series of breakdowns.

St Luke's, Woodside Park: Cheer up, think of all those poor people with operations.

Internees were vectored to my cell; they asked numerous questions. I was helping them with their careers, they didn't help my illness. I started a dreaded round of Psychiatrists, a sort of medical Paul Jones. Eventually I knew more about Psychiatrists and myself than they did.

There were those that did 10.00 a.m. to 5.30 p.m. when illnesses were supposed to stop. Those really great ones like Sydney Gottleib, anytime, anywhere, not so much pills as talk, bloody talk, even he would eventually run out of ideas and have to admit failure. In the end I decided that the Psychiatrist was a middleman for Roche. All the pills I took never cured the illness, they just clouded it. I was grateful for sleep-inducing drugs (having, of course, first been trained to take them; a touch of Pavlov's dogs). I had Seconal, Medinal, Sodium Amytol, Miltown Tofranil, Tryptazol etc, etc. Attending a new 'Shrink', I reeled off the catalogue of drugs I'd had. From a drawer he produced a piece of cardboard on which he had stuck (rather badly) the spectrum of mind pills.

'Which of these *haven't* you had?' he said desperately.

I had been seeing a very well known Psychiatrist an associate of R. D. Laing. One night he phoned me: 'For God's sake help me, my wife's having a nervous breakdown, I don't know what to do.'

I could end there. No, just a little more.

I have met Psychiatrists who are, in fact, nut cases. I had been trying to help an Anorexia case (love, understanding) when the looney contacted her and said: 'Come and live with me and my family in Cornwall and I will cure you.' Very poor, she borrowed the money from me to go. A week later he told her he'd 'had enough' and I had to bail her out. He's still practising.

The tragedy is, neurotics will believe anyone. I did, but as the dreary years of depression continued, I began to realise that there was no cure. In 1964, I concluded that like a malformed limb, you're stuck with it. The moment I faced up to this fact I felt better. I knew *I* had to handle the illness. All this along with advice from Sydney Gottleib: 'Exercise; the flow of blood to the head alleviates tension.'

I took exercise, it happened, the total concentration and exhausting qualities of Squash gave me one hour a day when I didn't think of anything but that little ball. Since that year I have improved 60 per cent, and I'm off drugs completely, and I haven't seen a Psychiatrist for ten years . . . I wonder where they've all gone.

George P Hare of Margate, 1927. (Frequently seen coming out of Mrs Vera Drell's house after dark.)

Muzak

The force-feeding of geese to produce pâté de foie gras is considered cruel (especially by the geese), but wait now, an adjunct of this appalling practice is upon the world. I am slowly being driven insane by a sort of musical dysentery (i.e. unstoppable shit) called Muzak – or piped music. Here in a world of energy crisis we have millions of kilowatts of energy being poured out for no real intelligent reason.

I have travelled the following airlines: BEA née BOAC née BA, now, wait for it! British (the same planes, the same staff, the same prices, but we *must* have a new name, more waste of energy), Qantas, Singapore (the worst), every airline down to the smallest, all indulge in the taped crap on take off and landing.

My daughter aged five said, 'Daddy, is this the pretend-we're-not-going-to-crash music?' Who are they kidding? Not only in aeroplanes, it abounds in nearly every restaurant, jean-shop, bar, pub, even in distant Australia. At the Vital Squash Centre, it is in every changing room, the showers, the loo (a good place for it). It's in the passageways to the courts, and you can hear it while you are playing. Outside you get into a taxi; *he's* got an equivalent pop station on. It's in the shopping centres, at the hotel, in the lift, it's everywhere. Now they say London Transport are going to have it on the buses. Now, if it was contributing towards a *need*, a request – OK. But no. It's there whether you want it or not; you're being 'Pâté Strasbourged', i.e. stuffed. The tragedy is, the ordinary (ordinary?) human takes it all. He is being emotionally indoctrinated. The moment it's switched off, he suffers withdrawal symptoms. In fact, it is identical to the Pavlov's

114

dog experiments. Now, if the people who heard this crap were *music lovers*, they would, like myself, resent it being forced on them. André Previn loathes it.

Gerry Mulligan, a superb musician, boarded one of the 'Singapore Airline torture' flights (Hot towels? grin; Sweets? grin; Folder of postcards? grin; Orange juice? grin; Socks? grin; Champagne? grin). He asked for the Muzak to be switched off. Switched off! SHOCK HORROR . . . Idiot air hostess reaction: Was this man insane? Switch it *off* – why it's against the airline's regulations (*sod* the passenger).

He asked the Chief Steward. Enter Chief, grin, Steward: 'Sorry, cannot switch off.'

Mulligan said, 'I paid to travel – *not* to be entertained.' So he unwraps his Baritone Sax and starts to play, whereupon the Steward reports this to the Captain.

I could go on – what's the use? The age of the trained idiot is on us. I actually carried out a poll. I asked each passenger in my cabin could he name or remember one of the tunes played on the Muzak. Not *one* could remember. Some said, 'What music?'

Here is an example of the arrogance of some people who allow this musical pollution. When in Australia I phoned the Lakeview Restaurant in Melbourne.

ME:	Excuse me, I'm trying to find a restaurant without that yowling piped music.
LAKEVIEW:	(*immediate resentment*) Well we do have piped music, yes.
ME:	Oh . . .
LAKEVIEW:	Well, it's very low, you can't really *hear* it (*Wow!*) they talk over it.
ME:	So, it's unimportant.
LAKEVIEW:	What is? (*How thick can you get?*)

I wanted to answer: a) the people talking
                       b) the Muzak
                       c) this phone call.

If logic is to be maintained, the reverse of the Muzak mania would be going to a Symphony Concert whereupon waiters rushed around and force-fed you during the concert.

I write this brief missive to show the pernicious eroding of the simple right of individuals to *choose* what they want in life, and to point out the billions of hours of wasted electricity used.

Myself and Douglas with Poochie his dog 6 years old. It bit the photographer (16 stitches).

Psychiatry

As a fulltime professional neurotic, who had been in and out of 'homes', I should call this article 'The man from the other side of the blankets.' Neurosis is a strange malady; one fluctuates twixt happiness and depression. Anything in between, which is called normal, is boring by comparison, mundane conversations grate on the nerves, but then clichés are the handrail of the crippled mind.

It's not that long ago that Bedlam was filled with people who were 'mental', chained to walls and if that wasn't bad enough, they were on exhibition to the public. Whole families on a Sunday would go along. Why? Why were people attracted to this spectacle? Because it *haunted* those who saw it; to them it was the inexplicable and therefore a mystery, and mystery had fascinated man since the beginning of time, so one can see how comparatively recent is the attitude to the 'insane'. I can't believe that had I lived at that time, I would have been one of those victims, and here am I writing about it.

Mental illness is to medicine what abstract painting is to art. There is no immediate cohesive logic and it is therefore baffling to the layman. However, the artist *means* something, but what? The mental patient too *means* something as well, but what? Initially, to the world of medicine, mental illness was disappointing: there was no blood, no breakages, no bruises and therefore, in the top ten illnesses, it was relegated to the bottom of the list. Not until the coming of Freud did it start to be treated and opened up what the world of medicine knows as Psychiatry.

What a mental patient craves above all, medicine apart, is *love* and

Enrico Pattzi, Leeds. (He is studying Greek here. He takes size 13 shoes, they and the rent were killing him.)

understanding. The greatest virtue I can recommend to the Doctor or the nurse, is patience.

There are two parallel lines to the neurotic, and I say neurotic as against totally insane. The neurotic personality is either created by environment or the condition is inherited. In my case it was both, I came from a highly strung mother and father. Neither was neurotic, but the symbiosis of both of them, created the right emotional humus for me to become one. This was brought about by an overbearing over-protective mother, yet, and this is interesting, my brother brought up the same way is normal. However, whereas he never, unlike myself, has had a breakdown, when he is under stress he breaks out in a psychosomatic rash ... I'm not quite sure what this signifies, I mention it that some research student reading this might try to interpret it. There is something most strange about neurotic malaise, in my case manic depression. As time went on I realised that it had benefits. For instance, when I was a patient at Woodside Park Hospital, Muswell Hill, in 1956, my mental equilibrium was totally shattered, but, my emotions were doubly alert. Morning birdsongs almost moved me to tears. I found it therapeutic; everything in my room seemed to come at me with a new vibrant life. The chair in my room seemed to blaze with life. Huxley in his *Doors of Perception* had exactly the same reaction to a chair when he took Mescalin, and I ponder if that is what made Van Gogh paint the chair in his room at Arles. My wife bought me a cassette player with some Chopin tapes. Although I had heard them before, now I found them exquisite.

What I'm saying is: if you have the right intellectual personality mental illness can be a strange bonus. Under the influence of it, I have written two books of poems.

So far I've been writing from this side of the blanket about the illness. How about the relationship with the Psychiatrist, the nurse? Like all living creatures, each one is different. Those with a wide spectrum of emotions got nearer to me and the illness, others failed to reach, move or convince me. Psychiatrists reach out to *try* and understand, but inevitably revert to tranquilisers or sedatives, Tofranil, Medinal, Seconal, Tryptazol all these and many more were thrust on me. They did sedate me; sometimes they turned me into a

Zombie. I know the Psychiatrists meant well but then so did Hitler. I'm not condemning the treatment. It did get me over sticky patches and continues to do so, but it hasn't cured me, and I accept that I will never be cured. Like Quasimodo's hump, I'm stuck with it. Having come to that conclusion I find it easier to handle.

To Mrs Lunge from 'Windy' (6 months)
who caused the divorce.

Police

There are two species of Briton: those for the police and those against. I'm one of the fors. That's why I'm writing this article for a fraction of my normal fee! (You fool, Milligan.) I'm suggesting that those pro-police citizens should be allowed four free crimes a year:

1) One egg allowed to be thrown at a politician of one's own choice.
2) Kicking any Iranian student in the backside.
3) All-day parking on a double yellow line outside the Bunny Club.
4) A free raspberry at any member of the Royal Family for grouse shooting.

First, the funnies. True police stories of old England. A rainy night in London, traffic snarled up in Leicester Square. Traffic lights broken down, lone policeman trying to sort it out. Me desperate to find a parking place. As I drew level with a bobby, I said, 'Officer, do you know a good place to park?' His reply: 'Sweden.'

And again, what police force addresses the highest to the lowest with equality. In Bayswater (Saudi-Bayswater). A wretched Scots football drunk lying in the gutter reeking from every orifice and sick all over him is addressed by a police officer as 'Sir'.

Another occasion, having traced a dog that fouled the pavement, I reported it to the Harrow Police Station. I was informed that one of our officers has cautioned the animal.

Peter Sellers in his black Mercedes dressed as an SS Officer with me in the back done up as Hitler. Sellers sees a young constable fresh from Hendon, pulls up and asks him: 'Zer, excuse me please, officer, but vere iss zer Cherman Embassy?'

'I'm sorry, Sir, I'm a stranger round here.' Touché!

I don't know why people in our cities don't take more advantage of our bobbies. No one ever seems to talk to them, except tourists. When I see a bobby on the beat or outside some forbidding embassy, I always try and have a word with them. Of course, I've had my moments.

Peter Sellers was always a gadget maniac. He had a device in his flat that connected with the Highgate Police Station. It was an innocent looking button that hung above the bed like a light switch. While he was away on tour I had reason to sleep in his bedroom. Reading in bed I pressed what I thought was a light switch. Five minutes later what looked like the front of the police rugby team burst in on me. It took phone calls, explanations, swearing on the bible before they released me.

The same week I was working late writing a deadline script. Three in the morning, gasping for a fag. Desperate, I go to Peter Sellers' dustbin, I know he leaves dog-ends three inches long. The beam from a policeman's torch illuminates me on my knees gibbering with nicotine, crowing and grubbing in the rubbish.

'Mr Raffles, I presume,' says the constable.

Of course, I've met police villains who are in it for a punch-up. An Inspector called to an 'affray' at Hammersmith gave me a truncheon, invited me to come along and 'join in'.

To the Irish Police. I was in a small Irish country town – the wife had gone into a shop to fill the thermos when a tall Polis'man approached.

'You can't park dere, Sur,' he said.

'I won't be a second, officer, I'm not obstructing any traffic.'

That someone had talked back overwhelmed him. He paled, frowned, coughed and started again.

'Did yez not hear me, den? You can't park here.'

I explained I wouldn't be more that a minute, I was a tourist etc. He stood thunder-struck – tears welled up in his eyes – then with

Nutts.

'Our Nutts showing his balls.'

123

desperation in his voice he said, 'Fer God's sake, drive on man,' and ran away.

Again, cheeky-bugger-police. I was driving on the M1 and to my horror I hear the police siren. A police car waves me down. What was it? Was it that girl's bicycle saddle I felt in 1939? The kids' money box? A tall, elegant policeman says, 'You were doing eighty, sir.'

'It wasn't me, officer, it was the car.'

'Just give us your autograph, sir.' End of chase.

Turning to the serious side of the police, I am very aware how the force has escalated in importance since the war. There was a time when the crime world and the police, in an unwritten law, forbade firearms. Alas, those days are gone – despite the fact that policemen on the beat are unarmed. One has the feeling that a bobby patrolling at night would feel much safer were he armed; this is the result of thugs who have taken to carrying firearms, that and 'we're-going-to-save-the-world' lunatic revolutionaries.

The current crop are Arabs, who are into street and embassy killings in a big way. I would like to pose the question: how do they get arms into the country? When an Englishman can be imprisoned for carrying one, it seems incoming foreigners get them with impunity. Isn't it time that the Diplomatic Bag was subject to X-ray scrutiny? It would not affect secret documents – and it would suppress the trade in illegal firearms.

I reflect that not many professions are as arduous and dedicated as the police. At any time of the day or night an ordinary British bobby can be confronted with an armed man. People like the SAS get special pay for that sort of confrontation. I wish the public would be more aware of the everyday risk that the average bobby takes.

I was one of those that was saddened at the split that took place during the Hippy flower-power era and has its hang over with punk/ Black Youths today.

I remember a confrontation at the Notting Hill Carnival between police and crowd, and an angry copper shouted, 'All right, next time you're having your head bashed in – don't call a copper, call a punk.' It summed up the police's frustration point in contemporary society.

Police accept frustrations at the citizen level – but many a policeman

124

must bang his head against the wall when having grappled with and arrested a thug for, say, beating up a senior citizen, and some looney Magistrate then gives the accused three months at some detention centre where they learn to plant roses – and go home for weekends.

Confidence in Judges and Magistrates must be at an all-time low in the light of recent judgements. I know of a case of a brutal sadistic rape attack (not his first). He got nine years – with remission, he will be out in five. I remember the police officer's face as he heard the sentence. I thought he would burst into Gilbert & Sullivan's 'A Policeman's Lot is Not a Happy One'. But what would we do without you?

*'At front gate.' Mrs Zena Throttle, a retired coalminer.
Her family never knew.*

Catholicism

Trapped! That's what has happened to me. Trapped by the devilish cunning of the world's oldest Catholic – Eamonn Andrews! He has been whining to that poor overworked wretch, the Editor of the *Catholic Herald*, the only newspaper not owned by Rupert Murdoch! He'll never get his hands on this paper with topless nuns on page three, ah no!

How did Andrews know a) I was Irish and b) a Roman Catholic? Can a man have *no* secrets – because I have a crucifix above my bed and a publicity photo of St Patrick on my door – do people have to jump to conclusions? (Why can't people *walk* to conclusions – or take a bus to conclusions?) After this article, I won't be able to walk the streets without people whispering behind my back, 'That's Spike Milligan, he's a *Catholic.*'

Well, I admit it – I well remember those distant days in Poona, India, my mother, Florence, my Grandmother, Mary, both trembling, fearful Irish Catholics. At the sight of a priest or nun coming up the drive, I was stripped of my messy clothes and clad in communion white. The best tea service appeared and the butter was taken out of the safe. My Mother's and Grandmother's faces lit up with a divine light as they served tea to Father Alborghette – a handsome young Italian priest who tied with Rudolph Valentino for looks. It was he who confirmed me in broken English. He pronounced my name Tay-rens-o Me-ye-garn (Terence Milligan).

I remember at the tender age of six at the Church of Jesus and Mary in Poona, Mother Fabian, tall, permanently flustered, bursting with goodness, who, when I got my sums right, would say with almost emotional relief, 'God bless you, Terry, for getting them right.'

At every turn in my young life I was confronted with religion; in every room was a picture of the Sacred Heart, with the message that comes back to me down the years: 'I will bless the home in which this picture is shown.' In my mother's bedroom, a private altar, likewise, my Grandmother's. To this day I still have a small porcelain angel that graced it. On my bed was a rosary, the beads made from imitation Connemara Marble. Every morning my mother placed a picture of St Theresa in my pocket to protect me.

So, when I grew up I realised I had been indoctrinated into Catholicism. I felt I had been cheated of that gift of freedom – self choice. I was eighteen. The rebellion set in. It must have happened to millions of teenage Catholics. Atheism called and communism, those harbours of dissatisfied youth. It divided the family's *entente cordiale*. Sunday morning rows with my mother, who was the traditional blind-belief Catholic. The religion could do no wrong, how could it – God was a Catholic and possibly Irish as well – a watertight argument.

I had to consider the rift twixt me and my family. I considered winning over my brother Desmond, aged nine, but then I realised I would be doing what religion had done to me i.e. indoctrination before mature consciousness. So I remained in the wilderness right through World War II. Nevertheless in my Army Paybook I wrote: Religion – RC.

Yet I could not but admire my mother's devotion to her religious duties. Early Mass, Communion, feast days, all devoutly observed, the bedroom altar draped in purple at Easter, the fish on Fridays, the attempts at leading a good, clean Christian life, and I had to admit that my own principles, non-smoking, teetotaller, non-promiscuous lifestyle had been handed to me by a Catholic environment, and I had to admit that my non-religious atheist friends were the direct opposite. I discovered I was now swearing like a trooper. I didn't like it but there I was.

All through the years I wrestled with, and re-evaluated the religion I had left. About the existence of God I could find no evidence nor, for that matter, can anyone. So where does one begin? Jesus. He was

Judith Moriarty, a bullet tester, 1915.

real – the physical evidence of a divine. Jesus had been fed to me by well-meaning, simple-minded nuns, priests, brothers, and parents; Jesus was someone at whose mention, you fell to your knees, crossed yourself, bowed your head and emptied you mind, I had been brought up to think of him as a statue.

If I were to continue my story it would fill every page of this paper, so let's say I chose to return to Catholicism on my own terms. I found Catholicism *holier* than other Christian religions (though often blindly so). Apart from its archaic (over-population) stand on birth-control. It seemed the one religion I wanted though I'd preferred Jesus to have been a vegetarian. I made sure my children weren't fed religion mindlessly. I talked to them about Jesus as a real person, something I'd never had. I'm still not sure about God, but I'm not worried. Living a good, decent, Christian life is what's important. Live that life and the rest will follow.

This article is a plea to the Catholic religion not to go for numbers – go for quality.

Drinking Wine in Australia

Life is full of surprises, like a man wearing his glasses, suddenly couldn't see, the prescription had run out. The next surprise: *Sunday Telegraph Magazine* have asked me to write an article on 'Drinking Wine in Australia', 400 words; the trouble is I don't know that many. So I'll make up for it with words like Swonnicles, Zollock and Perdufkins. Why one has to go half-way round the world to drink wine in Australia must be a hangover from convict transportation days. 'I sentence you to drink Emu Burgundy for life in Van Diemen's land.'

It came to pass in 1956 I *was* transported. I was at Rudy Kumon's Art Gallery in Pitt Street, Sydney. I spotted a crate of red wine in his office.

'How much is that painting?' I said.

'Would you like to taste it first?' he said.

After half a bottle I said, 'This is a very fine painting.'

'Yes,' he said, 'it's a Leo Buring Coonawane Claret 1954.'

'54?' I said. 'The paint must still be wet.'

Swonnicles. Of course, as we all know, some wines are best drunk when young. That's why I started when I was seven. He opened another painting of Penfold's Cabernet Sauvignan 1953. It was delicious! Better than Picasso's Harlequin 1903.

It was the start of an adulterous affair with Antipodean wines. There were surprises. Being broke, I stuck to cheap New South Wales whites. In the historic Ayres House Restaurant, Adelaide, I asked the wine waiter, 'Do you keep Ben Eann?'

The Argghhh! family at a wedding reception, Scunthorpe.

'Not if we can help it.'

'All right, clever dick,' I said. 'What do you recommend?'

'Kangaroo tail soup,' he said.

'What year is it?' I said.

He looked at a calendar. '1954, everyone knows that.'

'Is it a good year?'

'Not for the kangaroo.' With that he opened a Seppelts Bin 57 Shiraz. 'Try that for size,' he said pouring it into a teacup. 'It's from the Barossa Valley.'

'Really?' I said. 'I didn't know they made teacups in the Barossa Valley.'

But seriously, folks, at my parents' home in Woy Woy my father introduced me to a delightful pre-dinner summer wine, Eden Valley Moselle, the equal of any German including Hitler. He followed this with an Orlando Blue Label which I can only describe as an Orlando Blue Label. Zollock. With a barbecued Barramundi stuffed with mangoes I was given a Montrose Chardonnay 1980. Here was a wine tasting better than its French counterpart!!!! No wonder the convicts never came back! Next, after a Pavlova made in the shape of Dame Edna's leg, came a Brown Brothers 1979 Sauterne. Wow! It was like being covered in fudge sauce and licked clean by Elizabeth Taylor.

But to the greatest wine in Australia. One night I dined with Oz artist, Sir Tass Drysdale. 'This wine shouldn't be drunk. It should be injected with a hypodermic into the thigh.' So saying, he put on Shostakovich's Seventh Symphony, threw back the curtains on a lightning storm developing across the Pacific, then poured me a glass of Grange Hermitage 1964. One mouthful was enough.

'Like it?' he said. 'Now if Jesus had turned the water into that, they'd have let him go.'

Oh yes, there's a lot to be said about drinking wine in Australia and this has been some of it. Perdufkins.

Little Molly Drench with dog Wally.

How to Crack a Walnut

'How to crack a walnut without leaving your bed.'

I hear you ask, 'Who would want to?' or 'Ah! its a device for a cripple or a bedbound invalid.' Wrong! How to crack a walnut without leaving your bed is for the 100 per cent fit person.

I hear you say, 'Can you get it on the NHS?' You see, cracking walnuts without leaving your bed is, in fact, a strange device drawn by the late W. Heath Robinson, the direct predecessor of Emmett and his weird machines.

I remember during my golden boyhood days in India, I must have been seven, when I opened a bundle of magazines from 'Blighty' and it was in the *Sphere* that I saw this insane drawing of the walnut-cracking machine. I thought it hysterically funny. It was my first introduction to that which is peculiar to the English, namely, eccentricity. Till then my sense of humour was governed by Pip Squeak and Wilfred, or the antics of Harry Wharton and Co. at Greyfriars, but suddenly the impact of W. Heath Robinson took me into the abstract fields of the absurd. But on inspection of his drawings it showed that more than likely, with a few modifications, these insane machines would work.

Proof of this was brought to life by a part of India Kipling never heard of (though he was actually a friend of Robinson). The major of my father's regiment, the 88th RFA, set up a competition for the farriers of the regiment to build a Heath Robinson machine of their own choosing. Our battery farrier, Leslie Eggit, conceived a contraption called a Hot Curry Modifier Mark I, meant to cool the mouth and body of those eating a Vindaloo. The victim was strapped to a platform on rollers with springs strapped on his boots and pushed hard up against some railway buffers, by the use of cotton reels, pulleys, ratchets, wire and string. The victim was fed a spoonful of vindaloo then immediately was shot along a rail to the other end where he was doused with cold water and a ball of crushed ice dropped into his mouth. Did it work, you will ask. The answer is yes, as my own father was the victim in this case. I remember the first prize was a book of Heath Robinson's drawings autographed by the great man himself, and that selfsame book is now with my mother in Australia.

I hear you say, what of it? Well, the fact is that without ever knowing it, Heath Robinson pointed me and my sense of humour in his direction. There was a lot of his imagery in the Goon Show. Likewise, I was delighted when, in 1978, Hutchinson approached me to set to verse thirty-six of Heath Robinson's drawings of Goblins.

In conclusion I can but applaud the Chris Beetle's gallery on their exhibition of Robinson's work. I hope it appeals to a new generation, and, who knows, it might spark off some young minds . . .

Wally, a moment after Molly had gone.

My Christmas Read

William Shakespeare, Francis Bacon, Robert Graves, Jim Godbolt, which is the odd man out? Jim Godbolt? Clever reader, go to the top of the class and jump off. No, but seriously folks, this brings us to *The Mail on Sunday*, a misleading name when we all know that no mail is ever delivered on a Sunday. However, I was delivered at 2.00 a.m. on a Monday. That's why my personal cognomen is The Male on Monday.

I have been asked to contribute to 'Who likes What'. Well, personally 'I Who likes What' have settled for a very unostentatious little book by the aforementioned Jim Godbolt called *All This And Many a Dog*, sounding like a mispronounced Samuel Beckett play, *All This And Many A Waiting For Dogo*. However, it turns out to be a delightful little book telling us how Jim Godbolt, one of nature's losers, wandered into the world of Jazz music eventually becoming an agent. He handled drunken Jazz musicians of the calibre of Mick Mulligan to an aging 1930s band leader, Bert Ambrose. Godbolt is so successful at this that he ends up as a meter reader for the London Electricity Board being bitten by many a dog in the process. Finally he ends up as Editor to the Ronnie Scott Jazz Club house magazine.

The book gives us the whole spectrum of post-war Pop music to the explosion of the Beatles and the demise of the big bands, written in an easy, conversational tone with no mention of AIDS or the Royal Family. A very interesting read.

137

Mrs Tessa Thudds wearing a dead fox.

Miss Edith Teeth wearing a mattress.

National Maritime Museum

Help. I am drowning – this is the sort of cry that people in their right mind give off when they have fallen in (a) a pond, (b) a lake, (c) the ocean, and (d) if they are a dwarf, the bath.

People who go below the level of water are called (a) drowned (b) dead, these both have an equal rating. Now, how to stop drowning, the simple answer is to abolish (a) ponds, (b) lakes, (c) oceans and (d) if you are a dwarf, baths.

Local councils have managed to destroy ponds and they have managed to acidify lakes, so that you are perfectly safe from drowning in an acid lake, but the flesh will erode to the bone in 30 seconds. If you are good humoured it can be called slimming, otherwise dead; so that just leaves the seas and the oceans as a permanent menace to man. Man, to get across these oceans invented swimming, followed by exhaustion, and the newly discovered drowning. So, the problem was to prevent drowning in water. The best way to prevent this appeared to be to stay above it. There appeared to be no evidence of drowning on dry land. So many had heard of Jesus walking on the water, and, of course, this seemed an ideal and cheap way to transport oneself from, say, Dover to Calais. Somehow, despite repeated attempts, nobody could pull it off like Jesus.

Something had to be done. Clever men observed that when they threw their stick into the sea for the dog to retrieve, the stick remained afloat. So, man started to travel on the sea by stick. He made one fatal error; the stick had to weigh more than the man. He observed during the annual floods that trees that coagulated together on the

140

surface of the river could be walked on with a degree of safety. Yes, travelling by log had arrived. Wait, no – whereas man could sit astride the log, it remained stationary in the water, and many died of starvation waiting for the log to motivate itself, but some clever Dick, or it could have been Harry or Jim, invented logarithms. By tying logs together they found out that you didn't fall in between them. So, now they had a whole raft of logs which would float and which they could stand on, but with the same trouble, they stayed still.

Occasionally a light breeze would blow up, this would enter the voluminous togas, underpants and knickers of the raft dweller, and this would caress it forward across the bosom of the ocean. (This word bosom is very suspect, I have never seen any ocean that looked like a bosom. For a start, if for instance it was like the late Mae West's, it would mean travelling uphill on water, and a rapid descent down the other side.) These winds passing through men's underpants were (a) to bring about a certain degree of pleasure, and (b) to herald the coming of the sail by hanging up all their laundry on a washing line aboard the raft, which immediately propelled the vessel in the direction of away. This restricted travel inasmuch as it could only happen on drying days. All scholars of the Tall Ships will know that what followed in the wake of those floating drying platforms, apart from sharks and fag ends was the realisation that more clothing on the drying line meant a greater turn of speed (my turn for the speed next week).

So, as much clothing as possible was added to the line, and of course, this resulted in nude sailing.

What I have told you is the basic principle upon which the great wooden ships came into being. This led to the early Triremes which broke all the rules. These were the Greeks, who must have been looneys, for they no longer travelled by laundry. They used lumps of wood with splayed ends which they called oars; so with it vanished the art of sailing by laundry; but along with the Athenians, Persians and Medes, the result of straining at 100-foot long oars, led to a new Naval discovery: double rupture, piles and hernias, and it wasn't long before we again saw socks, vests, underpants and petticoats driving these noble ships along.

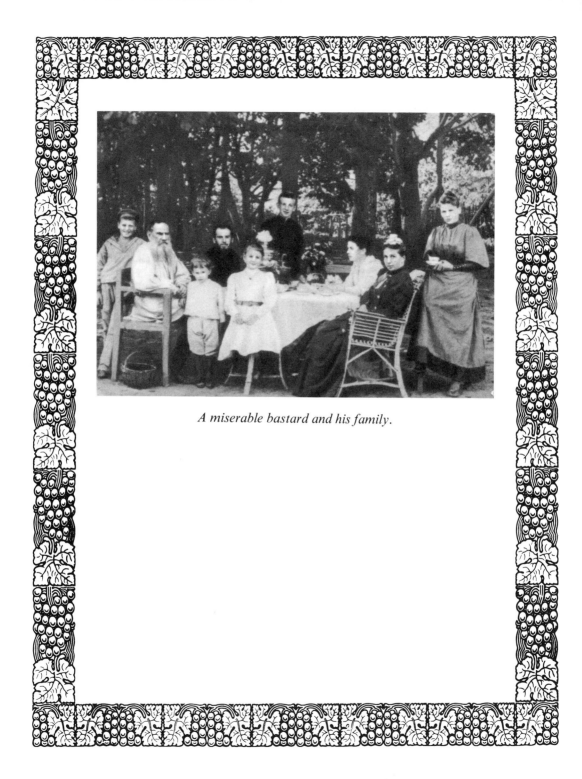

A miserable bastard and his family.

Now the Phoenicians (early Marks and Spencers) who did all the cutting of the underwear, vests and knickers, started to make them in kit form; you would get 50 by 80 foot sheets of cotton all stamped out for the factory to cut out the patterns to display these great sheets of underwear, by hanging them from a cross post, under a long pole, on one of their ships, hence the word 'Summer Sails Starting Today' (the word has since changed to sale, owing to saving one's eyes). Needless to say these great sheets of underpants and knickers blossomed out in the great spinnakers and mizzentops, such as we saw the Americans sweating over when they lost the America's Cup.

Basically, folks, what I am saying is the result of all this early history can be seen at the National Maritime Museum. For me the wonderful showpiece is the Cutty Sark. If for nothing else, go and see this incredible masterpiece of the Shipwright's artistry, the sheer grace and elegance of it and the harkening back to days when the word romance meant you were at sea and under sail.

Take the wife, take the kids and take the Granny, but just in case there's a high wind hang on to your underwear, because that's how it all started. If you want a meal and a drink the historic Trafalgar Tavern is adjacent where Charles Dickens went for his whitebait.

Holiday Package

There was a honeyed time when through the impoverished eyes of my early post-war years, the nearest I got to the exotic holiday, was through a Travelogue at the local flea pit, or the glossy travel brochures that were starting to proliferate with the coming tourist boom. One day, I thought, I will make enough money to go to a sun-scorched beach, and splash in turquoise waters. Well, what do you know? It all came true. I worked hard, money was shovelled into my coffers, and the world was my oyster.

Wrong! Had I only gone on dreaming. Alas, I found the conditions in the glossy brochure better than reality. I first settled for 'Historic, sunladen, land of the Lotus Eaters'. So said the brochure.

I arrived at Goulette Airport Tunis, destination Skanes Palace Monastir. The Glossy Brochure Car – 'Will meet you at the airport and waft (yes, waft!) you to your destination' – did not materialise. What did materialise was one hour of argument with the tour rep, during which a Tunisian customs officer tried to confiscate my radio/cassette player believing that the reason for my trip was to sell it!

Finally a taxi turned up, who, having us by the shorts charges us double for the trip. The 'Delightful bungalow on to the sea' had delightful non-functioning air conditioners, so we slept with every window, and door closed at night to avoid malarial mosquitoes. It was like sleeping in a sauna, I won't warn tourists of the minor irritations, but we made a visit to Ras Domas (Roman Thapsus). I and my wife were looking over the ruins, when three Arab youths with spear-guns threatened us with violence. It was very frightening. I wrote to President Bourgiba, and despite a second letter, I was ignored.

Had enough Milligan? No, this was just a one off. Next glossy brochure holiday – 'Greek villas in historical Lindos'. This turned out to be a cupboard with a fridge. At dawn it was a rat race for three-wheeled motor vehicles to awaken you. Every afternoon during siesta it was noisy. Greek men sat under our window and spoke as though conversing with the deaf. At night, across the bay, four discos blared out appalling Quadrophonic music which continued until 4.00 a.m. We searched out isolated beaches, only to find them so fouled as to be unbearable. I prayed for the day I flew home.

What's that jolly British Airways tune? 'We'll take good care of you'. Well, something must have gone wrong. From the roof of the plane water kept dripping, the carpet underfoot was soaked.

'It's the condensation,' explained the helpful Air Hostess.

Surely this was just a run of bad luck? One more time. Comes 1980, year of hope, and this time it's gotta be good. My Auntie has recommended us a villa in Corfu. The brochure looks good; I speak with the agents, all charming helpful, quiet, yes, isolated, yes, own catering etc, fine. There's the usual cattle round-up flight, OK Corfu. Most dangerous airport in the Med, says helpful fellow passenger. Hire car OK. Off we drive to Kassiopi. Our villa is isolated, the views are superb, Albania. Villa a converted farmhouse, no luxury but comfortable.

Shortcomings occur as time passes. Half the light bulbs are dead; 'Sorry no replacements, we have to get them from England.' (Then why don't they?) Water pressure not very good. Why? Water is from well, well is nearly empty.

'I'll get a water wagon to fill it up.'

'Daddy, Daddy, the toilet won't flush.'

Daddy can get it to flush, no he can't. What Daddy can do is fight a burst pipe which is flooding the house, and he only succeeds because he brought a) a kit of tools, and b) adhesive waterproof tape.

Eating out in Kassiopi, very nice if you can stand appalling Western

145

Councillor Jim Frogs with Mrs Chambers (Violin) and
Nora Trifles (Harmonium) and Rover.

Rock music, full blast, not one tune mind you, but five tavernas, cheek by jowl, each with a different tune.

Conversation is impossible. The tourists don't seem to mind as they appear to be pissed out of their minds. Young trainee rapists with tattoos from their ankles up to their teeth shout 'Whey oop, Spike, can I have your autograph on this fag packet?'

So, meals at home for Daddy. Never mind, there are those glossy 'Golden Beaches', but, not apparently on Corfu. There was every kind of filth on the beach except dying lepers. A fortnight's holiday in the Gents' Urinal at Victoria Station would be preferable. There were, of course, the intermittent electrical black-outs. The best surprise were the electrical shocks from the water taps. Nothing like 200 volts in the bath with a wet body. A search revealed an earth wire wound round the water pipes. It was hell having to bath in rubber gloves and plimsolls.

The Chiselhurst Laundry Workers' annual outing.
Scunthorpe 1928. Left to right: Maud (starcher),
Ivy (ironing), Olive (sheets).

Australian Relics

A year ago, whilst performing in Adelaide during the Festival, I took a week off to go fossicking for Colonial architectural relics. During this search I came upon what must have been some of Australia's earliest graffiti. It was at the Church of St James a few miles out of Adelaide at what was the Colonial settlement of Blakiston. It was a typical Colonial church of the period, the foundation stone of which had been laid on 3 October 1846, completed and consecrated in 1847 by Bishop William Short (the first Bishop of the Diocese). Built of local honey-coloured sandstone it has remained unaltered (a miracle?) to this day. Across the road is the shell of the village school. This also has suffered from the twentieth-century disease, vandalism. However, the walls are still intact and there is still hope (I reported its condition to the Australian National Trust).

However, it is to the graffiti that I return. Walking around the Church, I noticed on the West wall a series of etched illustrations of tri-masted sailing ships. One had the name *The Dash*. Subsequent investigation at the Records Office brought to light that this ship and another, *The Dart*, were the two that brought out the early Settlers to the Colony, among them Captain T. Davison, who settled at, and named, Blakiston in 1840.

Along with the ships a score of names are engraved on the walls, some with professional skill.

An interesting one celebrates Queen Victoria's Jubilee. Unless your readers can prove to the contrary, I can only assume that the AGR mean A Glorious Reign.

A last note, the Church has been in continual use since its erection – perhaps, after all, God isn't dead.

149

Acknowledgements

The Author and Publishers would like to acknowledge the following publications, in which many of the articles in this book first appeared: *Antique*; *Barclaycard*; *BBC Wildlife Magazine*; *Catholic Herald*; *Country Life*; *The Countryman*; *Daily Express*; *Dictionary of National Biography*, Bodleian Library; *Doctor*; *High Life*; *Mail on Sunday*; *Penthouse*; *Police Review*; *Punch*; *Radio Times*; *Sunday Telegraph*; *Sunday Times*; *TV Times*; *Woman's Day*, Australia; *World of Interiors*; *Yorkshire Post*.

They would like to thank Mediasport, the National Maritime Museum and Shell Mex International. Thanks are due also to John Rolph for the loan of many of the photographs reproduced in this book.